Love Remains

A MERCY HOUSE NOVEL

Terry Tamashiro Harris

TORCH RUNNER
PUBLICATIONS

This book is a work of fiction. Names, characters, places, and incidents are the product of the author's imagination or are used fictitiously. Other than key organizations and a few individuals listed in the author's note, any resemblance to actual events or persons, living or dead, is coincidental.

Love Remains: A Mercy House Novel
Copyright ©2024 by Terry Tamashiro Harris

Published by Torch Runner Publications
An Imprint of Harris House Publishing
harrishousepublishing.com
Arlington, Texas, USA

Book Cover by Gen1 Creative

All Scripture quotations, unless otherwise indicated, are taken from the Holy Bible, New International Version®, NIV®. Copyright ©1973, 1978, 1984, 2011 by Biblica, Inc.™ Used by permission of Zondervan. All rights reserved worldwide. www.zondervan.comThe "NIV" and "New International Version" are trademarks registered in the United States Patent and Trademark Office by Biblica, Inc.™
Scripture quotations marked TPT are from The Passion Translation®. Copyright © 2017, 2018, 2020 by Passion & Fire Ministries, Inc. Used by permission. All rights reserved. ThePassionTranslation.com.
Scripture taken from The Voice™. Copyright © 2012 by Ecclesia Bible Society. Used by permission. All rights reserved.

ISBN: 978-1-946369-63-5
Subject heading: FICTION / WOMEN'S FICTION

Publisher's Cataloging-in-Publication Data
Names: Harris, Terry Tamashiro, 1969- author.
Title: Love remains : a mercy house novel / Terry Tamashiro Harris.
Description: Arlington, TX : Torch Runner Publications, 2024. | Series: Mercy house series, bk. 1.
Identifiers: LCCN 2024903710 (print) | ISBN 978-1-946369-63-5 (paperback)
Subjects: LCSH: Grief--Fiction. | Faith--Fiction. | Miscarriage--Fiction. | Mother-hood--Fiction. | Friendship--Fiction. | BISAC: FICTION / Women. | FICTION / Christian / Contemporary. | FICTION / Friendship. | GSAFD: Christian fiction.
Classification: LCC PS3608.A77 L68 2024 (print) | LCC PS3608.A77 (ebook) | DDC 813/.6--dc23.

For Chet with all my love,
and to those like him
who may have never had
a name on this earth,
but who left their mark
on the lives of those who loved them.
We are richer by far
for having had you even briefly.

Foreword

by Susan Hulet
Founder & Former Executive Director
of Mercy House Ministries, Inc.

Pregnancy is beautiful. Life is beautiful. But pregnancy and life can be really hard when you're single and facing it alone, particularly if grief or loss is involved. Terry Harris knows this and is no stranger to the practical hands-on kind of volunteering that every maternity home needs. As the founder and past Executive Director of Mercy House (the non-fictionalized one), I have seen Terry give countless hours of prayer and counsel, consistently loving and serving our residents. Her time faithfully ministering to our mothers has given her a unique, inside look at the activity and dynamics that work within a group maternity home like Mercy House. Terry has beautifully captured the heart of our mission, and the challenges of our residents and staff, in this most perfect and wonderful novel of love that remains.

Chapter 1

I never considered that I was running away. Just starting over. Fresh. But the moment the Uber rolled to a stop in front of the large wrought iron gate, I realized I had made it to the safe zone. The sanctuary. Mercy House.

As I stepped from the car, tears stung my eyes and a strange feeling swelled in my chest. What was it? Relief? Release? A glimmer of restored hope?

Peering through the scrolling ironwork of the gate, I drank in the beauty of the stately Victorian home. Intricate trim accented the high-pitched gables. Uniform balusters spanned the width of the porches and balconies. Mature rose bushes, heavy with blossoms, flanked the front steps.

I closed my eyes, letting the April sunshine warm my upturned face. The intoxicating fragrance of a wisteria vine infused the air. I filled my lungs to capacity and exhaled slowly. I could breathe again. Savoring the moment, I allowed myself to be fully present—no thought of what lay ahead, nor any glance behind. I was here. Finally, here.

The crunch of car tires on loose gravel startled me from my reverie, and I spun to see the driver pulling away.

Gratefully, I noted that he had stacked my luggage beside me.

Sucking in one more breath, I pressed the button on the gate speaker. A circular camera lens turned blue, making me suddenly aware I was being watched. I tucked a loose strand of hair behind my ear. Hopefully, the Texas humidity hadn't brought out my wild frizz. My hair had a mind of its own. I normally tamed it with a hat, but a hat didn't seem appropriate for the first day at my new job. I had also forgotten to put on lipstick before I left the airport. In my opinion, the only difference between scary hair and glamorous waves was the polishing effect of lipstick. Typically lipstick wasn't my vibe though, so I preferred hats of all types.

Fidgeting, I stared at the blue circle. "Hello?" I said. "Is someone there?"

Maybe they weren't answering on purpose. I must have looked pretty haggard, having left Boston so early. I was up at 3a.m. to get to Logan in time for my 6a.m. departure. And of course it was a cheap flight, taking two layovers to finally make it to DFW. Now, the white pressed blouse and tailored blazer I had picked for a first impression didn't seem like such a great idea. But thankfully, the stretch fabric ankle pants retained their shape no matter what.

The gate speaker emitted a muffled rustling noise and then a woman's voice. "Uh . . . yeah. If you're selling something, we're not interested."

Well, that was unexpected. Double-checking the house number, I tried again. "This is Elle . . . Eleanor Anders. I'm the new Client Care Manager."

"Oh! Okay."

Okay . . . ? Nothing else. I waited a moment, expecting the gate to open, but it didn't.

"Um, hello?" I said again.

There was static or shuffling, then the woman's voice, "Yep. Still here."

What kind of reception was this?

With a flash of panic, I realized I had upended my whole life for this. Stay calm, Elle. But I couldn't stop the desperate hope that Mercy House was all I dreamed it would be. Waiting another moment or two for a response, I spoke again.

"Denise Stratton asked me to arrive today." I tried to conceal the alarm I felt rising in my chest.

A static hum told me the speaker was on again, and I thought I detected whispers and shushing. "Okay. I'll buzz you in," the voice said finally.

Was that a squeal I heard before the speaker cut off?

You're not giving in to negative thoughts, Elle. I shook my head clear as the large iron gate jerked awake and slowly rolled open. Strapping my large duffel over my shoulder, I steadied the smaller one on top of my wheeled suitcase, maneuvering carefully over the gate track.

Anxiety melted away as I made my way down the asphalt drive. I hadn't known quite what to expect of this place, but something in the wide front porch with its gracefully turned posts seemed to speak the word, "Welcome." Even the ferns, dangling in baskets from the gingerbread trim, waved their greeting as they swayed in the breeze. The porch itself was like a beautifully scripted invitation, promising peace and rest. Wicker chairs with plump cushions practically begged me to sit with a tall glass of pink lemonade. *I will, I promise,* I mentally told them as I paused to drag my bags up the porch steps.

Before I could press the doorbell, the door swung open to reveal three young women whose expressions suggested they had been making prank calls at a slumber party. All three were dressed in loungewear, and one, who was obviously pregnant, even wore a bathrobe. The taller of the three stepped forward. She looked about my age. Her dark hair was slicked back into a short ponytail. A headband secured the shorter strands away from her face, causing her bangs to stick up like a feather headdress.

"Hi, I'm Rae," she volunteered. "Technically, we aren't allowed to answer the door—client protocol," she said, gesturing with air quotes. "But since the door is already open and you're supposed to be here, then I guess you could come in. You are our new babysitter, after all."

The other two girls giggled.

I cocked my head to one side and grimaced. "Is Denise here?" I asked.

"No," the pregnant one piped up. "She had to take Serena to the hospital. Early contractions or something. Not good . . ."

"Are any other staff members here?" I asked.

"Nope," Rae answered. "Ms. Sharon is on her way, but

until then, I'm in charge."

"You are not," the pregnant one laughed, giving her a playful shove. "You can't believe anything Rae says."

"That's not nice, Judith," Rae said sternly. "I'm going to have to put you in timeout if you don't watch your mouth."

I sighed. This certainly was not the reception I had imagined. I pushed my bags over the threshold as they parted to let me in.

"Oh, here, let us help you with those," Rae said, moving to assist me. "We can take them on up to your room."

"Thank you," I replied. "It's been a long day."

"You're telling me," Rae muttered, grasping two of my bags and heading toward the staircase. "Try waking up to a squalling baby three times in the night."

I bit my lower lip and hoisted the large suitcase by the handle as I followed behind. I knew coming here wasn't going to be easy. My friends told me it would be torture to put myself through this, and even my therapist had questioned my resolve. But I had to come. I knew Mercy House was part of my healing journey. I had to face it.

"Boy or girl?" I asked, glad that her back was to me.

"Boy. Name's Melvin. Two months old. He was born February 12th."

My stomach clenched. Melvin would be just one month younger . . .

I shook the thought from my head as I heaved the large case up the steps.

"How long have you been at Mercy House?" I asked.

"About six months. Came straight from the recovery center. You know the one? On Meacham?"

"No, I'm not from around here."

She swung around to face me as I reached the landing halfway up the steps. "Really? Where ya from?"

"Boston," I answered.

"Why would you want to leave Boston to come all the way to Texas to live with a bunch of hormonal women and crying babies?"

I shrugged. I wasn't willing to get into the details with her. "Because I believe in the cause," I said simply. "I admire the fact that you ladies chose to keep your babies even when abortion would have been an easy out. I just want to do what I can to support you all." Rae stared at me intently, silent, as if she were trying to scan my brain. "How about that room?" I prompted.

She turned around and continued climbing the steps.

I followed.

"You know we're a pretty fun crowd in spite of the hormones," she said. "And the babies, well, there are only two out of the oven right now. Although Serena could pop any time. I think you'll like it here. For what it's worth, I'm glad you'll be our babysitter."

A smile tugged at the corners of my mouth as I followed Rae up the worn, carpeted staircase. She continued to chat and I found myself relaxing as I took in the beauty of this grand place. It was an interesting feeling. My therapist helped me notice what types of things relaxed me. She had coached me to live in the moment, taking stock of what surrounded me so I could appreciate it.

I had always loved old houses and old things. In fact, before I settled on psychology, I studied interior design simply because I loved old homes and antiques. Just knowing they have a history—of highs and lows, joys and sorrows—inspires feelings of admiration and respect. Why couldn't people see people that way . . . recognizing that our experiences—both good and bad—make us fully formed, authentic individuals? Why couldn't we easily accept each other for who we are, the sum of those experiences—without judging whether that makes us good or bad?

Rae led me past a spacious landing with an antique settee and bookcase filled with parenting resources, Bible studies, and Bibles. Double glass doors framed the Juliet balcony I had seen from the street.

"You get the best room in the place," she said. "It even has its own private bathroom. Believe me, I begged to have this room that was sitting here empty while we've been crammed two to a room at times—Do you know what it's like to share a bathroom with three pregnant girls? But no-o-o-," she sighed dramatically, dropping one of my duffels in front of a paneled door, "it was reserved for the elusive client care manager." She turned the antique ceramic doorknob. "We've been waiting a long time for this position to be filled, but none of us knew you were coming today."

I peeked past her as she opened the door and dropped my other duffel inside. The curtains were drawn, but I could make out a high four-poster bed with a bare mattress. A large window dormer held a sturdy desk and chair.

"Rae!" a voice barked.

We both swung around at the sharp call. Determined footsteps clacked briskly toward us carrying a smartly dressed woman with a stern look on her face. "Rae," the woman said in a milder tone when she glanced at me. Her face contorted as her lips pressed together in a tight line like she was holding in a ticking bomb. "Rae, you have broken every protocol. Please go to my office, and we will discuss this."

"What was I supposed to do?" Rae shot back. "Leave our new manager standing at the gate until you got back?"

"Certainly *not* move her in!" the woman exploded. "I'm not going to discuss this with you here and now, but you apparently have jumped to conclusions again. This—Eleanor," she glanced at me again before returning her full fury on Rae, "is not the manager but is here for an interview!"

"What?!" Rae and I each responded, so closely that it sounded like an echo in a hall of mirrors.

That couldn't be right.

"There must be some mistake—" I said. "I was asked by Denise Stratton to report here today at one o'clock."

"I *am* Denise Stratton," the woman thundered back. "And it appears you have taken full advantage of our short-staffed situation."

"I-I—" My words caught in my throat at the horror of what she was implying.

"Hey!" Rae broke in. "Just calm down, Denise. I'm sure something got crossways—"

"YOU," Denise boomed, "do not tell me to calm down. Go downstairs now and wait for me in my office."

Rae shook her head in half-hearted concession and moved my other duffel into the room before she left.

My mind shot a hundred different directions as I tried to process what was happening. How could this have gotten so screwed up?

"I'm sure we can clear this up," I ventured. "Let me pull up the offer letter."

I fumbled for my cell phone to pull up the document that would clear this up.

"The email said my background check and references had been approved. It also had the amount of my starting salary," I continued, frantically typing in the search field on my email app. "I understood I was to arrive here at 1p.m. simply to complete the paperwork for a permanent position, residing on premises."

I stressed the last phrase because she had to understand I was moving here. I had no backup plan. Heat began to rise through my neck until my face felt flushed.

"The email you're speaking of was certainly not an offer letter," Denise said stiffly, obviously trying to regain control of her emotions. "This is a reputable ministry. We carefully vet every person who enters these doors because we are here to provide a safe place for our clients during their times of crises. I wrote that email," she said, her voice rising again, "and did so to clearly define the details. Yes, you passed your *initial* checks, and salary agreement is an important part of that, but there is much more involved in our hiring process than a few simple phone interviews."

"That was not clear in your communication." I struggled to keep my voice even, though the quiver was unmistakable. "I just arrived here directly from the airport. I've been on three flights, and a long car ride, and I have no other place arranged to stay."

"And you want me to let you stay here because you misunderstood?" Denise reached beyond me to pull my luggage out of the room and closed the door.

I had to be here. I couldn't go back. That was not an option. I would not go back. This was my sanctuary. It had to be. I felt my heart begin beating rapidly and I struggled to stave off a panic attack, trying my best to focus on slow, controlled breathing without making it obvious. Yet I could barely hear what Denise was saying over the pulsating beat reverberating in my eardrums.

Chapter 2

I willed my mind to focus on the terse words spewing from the woman who towered over me. "Our director, Sharon Rigby, will interview you in person," Denise was saying. "That's why you were to arrive at one o'clock. She will be here in fifteen minutes to meet with you."

When I spoke, my voice was barely a whisper. "I have been looking forward to meeting Sharon but was not prepared to do so under these circumstances."

"You may leave your bags here in the hallway." Denise eased her tone as if she sensed my distress. "Get what you need from them, and I will show you to the guest bath downstairs so you can freshen up."

Numbly, I stooped to dig my travel case out of the large duffel, then rose to follow Denise back downstairs. The wide foyer narrowed to a small dark hallway. She motioned me into a half-bath that apparently had been transformed at some point along this old house's history. It was much larger than a modern half-bath. A stained glass window filled the room with a violet glow, bright enough that I didn't bother turning on the light. The beauty of it soothed my frayed nerves. I moved to the antique pedestal sink. The mirror was marred around the edges where its silver had worn away with time. I met my gaze through its filmy, speckled reflection. A note of panic remained in my eyes. What would I do? Where would I go if I couldn't stay here? I had been so sure, so confident that this was the right thing. I thought I'd finally reached a turning point, getting my life back to where God wanted me to be. I thought he was directing me!

Angry tears sprang to my eyes. All my life I'd been told he works things together for good, and I was encouraged to follow his direction. But how was I supposed to know what that was? When I thought I was doing 'the right thing' where had that ever gotten me? I thought coming here to a Christian ministry would finally get my life moving in the right direction.

Bright pink blood vessels now covered the whites of my eyes. *And now I'm supposed to do an interview??*

Turning on the water, I let the cool stream flow over my cupped hands. How foolish I was to think coming here would make a difference. That it would matter to anyone, least of all God. Nothing I did ever seemed to matter. I could disappear and no one would be overly affected. Who cared? Why should I ever even try . . .

I shook my head. I could feel myself drowning, being sucked deeper and deeper until a suffocating feeling enveloped me. I knew these were lies. Lies that were pushing me down, deeper and deeper beneath the surface of rational thought. I recognized the same old tricks. Self-pity. At least that was its socially acceptable name. Really, it was selfishness, envy. Wanting that which I felt I didn't have. Believing that I wasn't enough as I was. Lies.

I took a deep breath and pushed my way back up to the surface. Gathering water in my hands, I doused my face. I would get through this interview. I would do and say what I knew, and whatever came out of it would be fine. I would be fine. If I didn't get the job, I would go on to something else. Just like I always did.

After drying my face on the hand towel, I took my toothbrush and deodorant from my case to freshen up.

Pull it together, Elle. You'll be fine.

I spoke to the distraught girl in the mirror with the authority of a coach, willing her to not quit, willing myself to believe she really would be okay.

* * * * * * *

I waited stiffly in a tufted armchair that faced an ornately carved desk. The room's paneled oak walls and antique bookcases provided a warmth I would normally enjoy. Instead, I strained to make out words in the contentious voices coming from another room. Denise's angry tone and Rae's defiant one mixed with another, gentler voice that I could only guess was Sharon, the founder of Mercy House. The one who would decide my fate.

Sharon was the entire reason I was here. I came across her TEDx talk on YouTube, and her words touched something deep inside me. A trained midwife, Sharon had devoted her career to helping women learn how to care for themselves and their unborn babies, specifically empowering pregnant women in crisis situations. Women who had no one to help them, who were considering abortion, and even those who had aborted or lost a child.

I devoured all her teachings. Her talk of hope, healing, and restoration invigorated me with new focus during my darkest time. Yet, it wasn't just her passionate words that inspired me; it was how she moved her cause forward, not content to sit idly by, but jumping in to provide practical help. She reached out to lonely, scared, rejected, abandoned, or abused women in their vulnerable time of pregnancy. Mercy House was born as a place to welcome those women, to come alongside them and teach them how to be good moms and equip them with all they needed for a fresh start in life.

Mercy House was a sanctuary. It was a calling. I wanted to put feet to my passion in the same way. Somehow my purpose, at least for this season of my life, was wrapped up here, and I needed to discover it. I knew I needed to be here. I needed this job.

The door opened, interrupting my thoughts, and I stood as Sharon walked in, her energy contrasting in a refreshing way with the maturity of her lined face. She was taller than I had expected, and her short shock of blond hair made her seem younger than she was.

"Elle!" she said, smiling warmly. "I'm so glad you're here."

Both of her hands clasped mine as I reached out expecting a formal handshake. A knot formed in my throat in response to her genuine warmth. Her smile and voice were so familiar, I resisted the urge to throw my arms around her like an old friend.

"I'm sorry that the circumstances which greeted you were less than ideal," she said, smiling sympathetically. "Hopefully, it only serves to underscore the need for this position to be filled."

"I'm not sure how the confusion happened," I said pensively. "I thought I had filled it."

"Well, this interview isn't as bad as it sounds," she said, waving her hand as if she were shooing away the unpleasantries of my arrival. "Consider it more of a getting-to-know-you session. I trust Denise completely in her decision-making, and by all intents and purposes, she has basically made the decision to hire you. However, this step has to come before she is willing to have final discussions with me. She is a stickler for processes and procedures, and that's what makes her so good at her job."

Sharon laughed good-naturedly, taking the seat beside me instead of on the other side of the desk. "Denise oversees the clients and staff and coordinates the ministries that come alongside Mercy House to help our ladies. She is excellent at that, but sometimes her focus on the details causes her to overlook the human factor in her approach. I'm sorry things started off badly between you two, but I can assure you that she is an amazing colleague."

Sharon must have noticed the skepticism on my face. She paused, motioning me to take my chair again. "I can make all kinds of excuses for her, including the crazy stress she was under today managing an emergency on her own, but we aren't here to talk about Denise. I want to hear from you." Sharon folded one of her long legs beneath her as if she were sitting down to chat with a dear friend. "Elle, I have to tell you I loved the letter you sent with your résumé," she continued. "I felt like I was reading your heart. There's a lot in there—your heart, I mean. Passion. Strength. Courage."

I felt myself relaxing and even offered a tentative smile. "Thank you."

"Tell me a bit about yourself . . . I know all the résumé stuff, but I'd like to know what makes you tick. What are your dreams, ambitions? What shaped you into the person of such intention I see before me?"

The old inner critic laughed, shaming me with the thought that outwardly I presented a person of intention while inwardly I was really a person running from pain, looking to survive the wasteland of despair. I hated the fact that this voice was plaguing me again. I had come so far, and now one potential crisis threatened to set me back. How could I let this happen so easily?

I shook my head, bringing my mind into focus. "Well, I grew up in Virginia. An only child. I had a bent toward psychotherapy from an early age. My mother struggled with severe depression. She hid it well, until she could no longer."

I took a deep breath. "Her illness, and her death, shaped me in many ways."

Did I sound like I was trying to garner sympathy, or worse, like I could have the same problems?

I hurried on, "I supposed it inspired me to go for a degree in psychology," I said. "But the interest in women's issues, specifically pregnant women in crisis situations, came much later. I found it interesting—and sad—that young pregnant girls were looked at with disdain while those who got abortions could go on with no outward repercussions because people had no idea they had been pregnant. I realized it was the brave ones who kept their babies, but I then discovered that those who had abortions weren't bad people. In fact, they suffered greatly afterward."

Sharon nodded and I cleared my throat, growing confident with the focus on my passion. "The underlying problem seemed to me that abortions were just too easy of an option," I said, "and that was simply due to the fact that the main people reaching out to ladies with unplanned pregnancies were the ones who performed abortions. Sadly, they don't tell the women about the emotional pain that haunts them for years after the loss of a child."

I thought about the first time I heard of a trash baby who had been born and thrown into a dumpster. My voice increased in intensity as I continued. "It's heartbreaking to me that women don't know their capabilities. Yes, you can be a good mom.

You just need someone to tell you that and someone to model that for you. It's frustrating that the Church has largely abandoned that role of offering grace and mercy, and instead seems to offer only judgment or apathy, washing their hands of women who find themselves in such situations."

I made a conscious effort to unclench my fists and soften my voice.

"I have witnessed sit-ins at abortion clinics," I said, purposely trying to be vague enough so she wouldn't know if it was as a picketer or a patron. I wasn't sure which one she would think was worse. "It always felt wrong to me. Here were women already confused and hurting. I know the group's intentions were against the clinic's practice, not the women, but the women were caught in the crossfire. Those hurting were the ones who felt the judgment." I paused again and exhaled deeply. "And then, as I mentioned in my letter, I heard you speak about Mercy House. It felt right. These women in crises need mercy, not judgment. Mercy House offers a safe place to be pregnant and learn how to be a good mom. I want to be involved in making a real difference in people's lives—not just the women who come here, but also their children, whose lives have the potential to take on a whole new trajectory."

Sharon nodded. "I love that you get it so well. I can see that you would work excellently at upholding our cause." She tilted her head thoughtfully. "People themselves can be a lot more difficult to uphold—we are all very human, and can be quite messy—and I'm not talking about physical messes."

She smiled and raised an eyebrow to see if I caught her meaning. Then her face softened with compassion as she continued. "These women come here very wounded and broken, often angry, sullen. Many come straight from drug rehab, some from sex slavery, many from abusive relationships. They can be very callous and hard because they had to be that way to survive. Tell me, Elle," she said, her eyes searching my face, "why do you want this role of working directly with the clients? What kind of difference do you hope to make here?"

I looked down at my hands. I had considered all of this. Honestly, I had somewhat glorified it, imagining myself as a Mother Teresa of sorts, coming in and winning their love and helping them stand on two feet again. But hearing it now from Sharon's lips, I wavered. I felt like my whole life was wavering . . . again.

Who do you think you are, imagining you could make any kind of positive difference to anyone?

Chapter 3

That voice. Back again. Why was it still so prevalent? Why couldn't I shake it? I thought I had learned not to give in to it, not to let it put me flat on my back in the bed, unwilling to move, unwilling to live. Yet, here I was suckered by it again.

Why was I even here? Why *did* I think I could help other people when I couldn't even seem to help myself?

Sharon's eyes searched mine as she waited for my answer. I knew she didn't mean the question in the same way the horrid voice in my head did. This woman's sincerity radiated from deep within her and somehow it gave me strength. Quickly, I reverted to the coping skills I knew by heart, recognizing the voice as something I could choose not to listen to, acknowledging the truth, and reminding myself of my strengths.

It was true that this would be a very difficult job. That was clear. But I had come a long way from the broken soul that would have crumpled at this question just a few months ago. I had helped myself. I was in a healthy place. I was prepared.

"You know my degree is in psychology," I began hesitantly. "And I worked the hotline for a crisis pregnancy center. I do have some experience in dealing with clients firsthand. As I put in my résumé, I had an internship in a psychologist's office during my last semester . . ."

Sharon nodded, waiting for me to go on. I knew she was probing deeper.

I cleared my throat again, buying time while I weighed my answer. I wasn't prepared to have an interview that exposed personal issues, but with this type of work, I realized they needed to know everything they could about the person they were hiring to live on-site. Denise was right. Mercy House was a place of refuge because of the stringent things they put in place to protect their clients.

I smiled wryly. "You ask some pretty hard questions . . ."

Sharon laughed. "Well, you know, we don't shy away from hard things around here," she said.

Taking that as a cue, I swallowed hard and plunged ahead. "In this past year, I went through a very hard experience . . . life-changing, actually." I paused, searching for the right words. "The experience caused me to question many things . . . including what I was living for. It was a very dark time for me. I realized that I had been very self-focused and I wanted to change that. That's when I volunteered for a bit at a crisis pregnancy center. I came across your teachings then and learned about Mercy House. Your teachings inspired me to finish my degree in psychology so I could work directly with women in crises."

I took a deep breath and continued. "For personal reasons, I needed to make a clean break from Boston, and when I saw this position, I knew it was what I wanted to do. This is a new season for me. A new life, really. I want it to count for something bigger than myself. I'm passionate about the work Mercy House does. That's why I want to work directly with the clients. I hope to inspire them like you've inspired me. I want to make a difference, and I know that will not be easy."

I could feel myself trembling, and I hoped it didn't show. People used to tell me how much they admired my strength and focus, my ability to jump in and make things happen, but now . . . I was different. I had learned to function as the new me, but I missed the strength and composure I once had. I had worked so hard over the last few months to keep the emotions in check, but they were all still there, bubbling just beneath the surface.

Thankfully, Sharon didn't seem to notice. She went on to explain what client interaction would look like on a day-to-day basis and what my responsibilities would be should I receive the role. I half-listened as I struggled to move my mind back to the present, but I felt like my research and previous interviews with Denise had given me a good grasp of the way things ran here. I had no question in my mind that this was where I needed to be. I hoped and prayed in a cross-my-fingers sort of way that they would see that too.

"How do you feel about that?" Sharon asked, catching me off guard as she pulled her monologue up short with a question.

I tried to cover up my deer-in-the-headlights expression. "I'm sorry, can you restate the question, please?"

"The Christian aspect of our organization . . . Can you

tell me more about how your values align with ours?"

"Well," I said, buying time to contemplate my answer. "Judeo-Christian values are the bedrock of our society; I believe every governing body does well to employ them as a guiding force." I paused, debating whether to leave it at that diplomatic answer or admit a fact I usually held like a dark secret. After a quick thought, I opted for the latter, recognizing it could provide the bonus points needed to clench this job. Inhaling deeply, I rattled off the words like I was running from a snake. "I grew up in a Christian home and was taught Christian values from as early as I can remember—my dad was a pastor."

I sat back in my chair and waited, watching Sharon's face turn from surprised to impressed. Satisfied, I quickly dismissed the twinge of guilt I felt for leaving off my ten-year estrangement toward my Christian roots. Honestly, I liked the fact that Mercy House was a Christian organization. It seemed to embody the best of what I felt Christians should be but often weren't.

"So, you are fine with attending church with the clients each Sunday?"

I cringed inwardly.

I had noted that the duties of this role required taking the clients to church, but I had hoped that didn't mean staying with them. I hadn't been to church regularly since I left for college and was gratefully free from the monotony of the Sunday morning routine. A familiar wave of nausea swept over me. It had often gotten me excused from going. But I pushed it aside now. I had to.

"Of course." I forced a smile.

"There is one more thing we need to probe deeper into, Elle." I stiffened at her words. "We noted in your background check that you are married, yet I assume you know this position on-premise is for a single occupant."

My face must have registered my shock. I couldn't even put together a coherent response.

"I know it seems unconventional that your place of employment would need to know personal details," Sharon hurried on, "but because our clients are often leaving abusive relationships, we keep Mercy House as secure as we can." Her eyes held mine. "It's important that we know if there are similar extenuating circumstances with you."

Ethan abusive? My lack of response probably set off alarms in Sharon's mind, but I couldn't formulate an answer.

My mouth opened and then closed, and for a moment I could only stare back at her. I hadn't expected questions about my marriage. Yet, what shocked me most was the reaction I felt about a person I had loathed for the last seven months. My defenses instantly shot up. It was almost habit. Ingrained, I supposed, from years of defending his character to my father.

"He's a good person!"

"But he's not a Christian, Elle!"

"He's a better man than any Christian I know!"

I knew that was a slap in my dad's face, but I was tired of him always invoking God in our arguments.

"The Word says, 'You shall not be unequally yoked.'"

I hated when he used the Bible against me. The 'sword of the Spirit,' as he called it, to 'war against the enemy of our souls.' Yet he used it to cut me to pieces as if I were his enemy. It happened over and over, but that particular time was the last time I talked to my dad, except for the voicemail I left when I confessed I was pregnant and getting married and that he should be proud of me for doing the 'right thing' to make a family for this new life growing inside me.

He never called back.

I shook my head clear of the past and focused on the arm of the chair I was sitting in. Consciously, I relaxed my grip on it and let my thumb soothe away the anxious thoughts against the velvet upholstery.

Finally, words came. "In answer to your concerns, I'm not leaving an abusive situation." I paused and willed my eyes to meet hers. "I do intend to live on the premises. My . . . uh . . . my husband and I are separated."

The sympathy in Sharon's eyes was palpable, and I had to look away.

"I'm sorry," she said. "That must be difficult for you."

I shrugged, avoiding her gaze. "It is what it is."

My emotion toward our marriage had grown numb months ago, replaced only by a lingering coldness. The coldness had led me to fill out the divorce application online, but I had yet to submit it. Having a conversation with Ethan was the right thing to do before he was served divorce papers, but I just couldn't bring myself to talk to him yet. Too afraid the emotions would return. The overwhelming sadness. Hopelessness. Despair.

I shook my head. "That's part of the reason I wanted to leave Boston. I'm looking forward to a fresh start. A new perspective." I tried to make it sound positive, not like a needy soul running away. I paused, searching for words to clarify, but not willing to divulge too much. "As a result of the difficult time we went through so early in our marriage, we just . . . floundered as a couple . . . needed space. I moved out a few months ago and haven't spoken to him since."

That moment played in my mind as a film where I was the spectator. The anguish on Ethan's face. His tears. As I watched the scene unfold, his pleading words were garbled, unintelligible, just noise to the closed ears of his wife as she shut the door behind her with no intention of returning.

"It just seemed best to break ties. He doesn't know where I am."

I lifted my eyes to meet Sharon's. Hers were sympathetic. She reached over and placed her hand on mine.

"Well, difficult circumstances certainly provide opportunity for re-evaluating things," she said.

She stood then and told me that she would have her discussion with Denise now so that I could settle my plans before nightfall.

* * * * * * *

The bedroom door clicked shut as Denise left me to myself. Sharon had been with her when she announced that the job was mine, although her tone told me I had not yet won her approval. The facts were that they desperately needed the help and I desperately needed the job. Whatever the reasons, I was grateful and thoroughly exhausted.

Numbly, I turned around and surveyed my new room. The high four-poster bed was now topped with a thick comforter and an assortment of pillows in subtle shades of green, ivory, and blush pink. The coordinating curtains had been opened, revealing the stark, smooth branches of a crepe myrtle tree silhouetted against the dusky sky.

I pulled my toiletry bag from my luggage and carried it to the ensuite bathroom, a luxury for a house filled with women. The clawfoot tub shower beckoned. Gratefully, I shed my stale traveling clothes and washed the day from my face and body. The hot water didn't last long enough for an indulgent shower, but I was happy to be clean. After pulling on my comfy pajamas, I began unpacking the rest of my things.

A knock on the door interrupted my task. Self-conscious of my pajamas, I opened the door only a crack.

It was Rae, the girl who was somewhat the cause of this entire upsetting day. If only she hadn't broken policy and answered the gate buzzer in the first place—I don't know what I would've done, but it wouldn't have been facing Denise's tirade. Although I knew that wasn't her fault, I couldn't help grimacing as I raised my eyebrows in question.

"Welcome gift," she said, holding out a package of candy. "Trollies make everything better."

"Thank you?" I questioned, opening the door to take the package from her. It was a nice gesture, and I felt my defenses lowering.

"Don't tell me you never had Trollies."

"I have no idea what that is," I confessed, examining the bright graphic of a neon worm on the front of the package.

"How have you lived this long without them?" she responded incredulously. "They're only the answer to your tastebuds' dream condensed into a single, squishy, scrumptiously sour gummy worm. You'll thank me when you try one, but you might hate me when you have to stand in front of a group confessing your addiction."

I felt my face relax into a smile. "I'll proceed with caution," I promised. "Thanks."

Closing the door, I tossed the gummy worms onto the bed and turned back to my task. One by one, I pulled out each item of clothing and hung it in the closet or neatly folded it into the chest of drawers. I emptied the bags of everything, except for the tiny, gift-wrapped box, which I left in the bottom of my suitcase.

When the last bag was stowed under the bed, the emotional roller coaster of the day came rushing down in a free fall. I flung myself on the thick down comforter and buried my face in the pillow to muffle the sobs that forced their way up from my gut in singular bursts of release.

It wasn't one thing I cried about—not the exhaustion, not the move, not the uncertainty, not the newness, not homesickness, not Ethan, and not even the little gift-wrapped package stowed beneath the bed. Rather, it was a torrent of nothingness. I felt nothing. Nothing at all except the threat of the deep, dark shadow that had tried to overtake me once more. But I had made it through. I had wrenched free from its snare and made it, finally, to the safe zone. I had escaped the monster of depression, for now at least.

As the sobs subsided, I rolled onto my side, wrapping the thick comforter around me. Something plastic stuck to my leg, and I reached down to peel it away.

Rae's Trollies. I wiped my eyes.

"Might as well see if they live up to the hype," I sniffed.

Opening the package, I pulled out a red, yellow, and green sugar-coated jelly worm.

"Not exactly appetizing, are you?"

I bit off its head.

An explosion of flavors rolled over my tongue.

Not bad. I stuffed the remaining three inches in my mouth. Not bad at all.

Maybe there's something to these Trollies.

I snuggled deeply in the blanket, feeling safe, even secure.

That was my last conscious thought before I faded into a deep, restful sleep.

Chapter 4

Wah! Wah! Wah! I stretched my arm from beneath the warm comforter, fumbling to silence my phone alarm on the bedside table. Strangely, the sound became louder, escalating into a full wail. Bleary-eyed, I sat up and surveyed my surroundings. I was at Mercy House! The sound was a baby crying.

I winced remembering the emotional mess I was yesterday.

Not today.

I threw back the covers. This was a do-over day. I was hired for the job, I was certainly capable of the job, and I would show Denise and everyone else that I was here to make a positive difference.

After washing my face and brushing my teeth, I pulled on my favorite jeans with a loose, lightweight sweater and low-heeled ankle boots. Brushing my hair into a low ponytail, I completed the look with a fedora-style hat. Most of my hat collection had been left behind, but I kept a few favorites—a Red Sox ball cap, a wide-brimmed straw hat, several beanies, and my favorite fedora.

My reflection grimaced at me in the mirror. And I had to agree. Somehow what constituted chic and trendy in Boston seemed very out of place in the Texas suburbs. I sighed and removed the hat. "We're not in Kansas anymore, Toto." I hung it on the bedpost and smoothed my hair, surveying myself in the mirror once more. Ready.

Sharon was at the stove, turning toast in a pan, when I stepped into the kitchen. She greeted me with a smile. "Good morning! How did you sleep?"

"Like a baby," I admitted with a sheepish smile. "I love the room you've given me."

Sharon laughed. "Our clients with newborns would probably disagree that the phrase, 'like a baby', means sleeping well."

"I hadn't thought of that," I said, laughing with her, as Rae entered the kitchen. She was still wearing pajamas.

"Morning folk, obviously," Rae muttered. Her bare feet padded against the wood floor as she went for the coffee pot.

Sharon looked at me and raised her brows, her eyes dancing with humor as if our previous exchange were an inside joke between the two of us. "Good morning to you, too, sunshine!"

"I'd rather not see sunshine for another hour." Rae poured herself a cup of coffee and turned to face us, leaning against the counter. Surveying me, she raised the steaming mug to her lips. "I see you're bright-eyed and bushy-tailed. Ready for your first day on the job?"

"Absolutely," I nodded. I actually felt better than I had in weeks. Excited even. I was in my element, back in my groove of expertise, a long, long way from the nervous, frazzled person I was yesterday. "I'm ready to learn the schedule and get going."

Rae pulled one of the hot slices of toast from the stack Sharon was making and took a bite. "Well, I just got Melvin back to sleep, so I hope you don't have plans to get us going until I've had a shower."

Sharon carried the plate of toast to the table spread with jams, fruit, and a meat and cheese tray. "Don't worry," she laughed. "Denise and I will keep Elle plenty busy today, so she won't give you marching orders just yet. Grab that pot of oatmeal off the stove, will you, Elle?"

I picked up the potholders and lifted the heavy pot as requested. "When does Denise get here?" I asked, carefully setting the steaming dish on the hot pads.

"She normally comes in at nine since she drives from the other side of the metroplex," Sharon answered. "For breakfast every day, it's just the clients and me and Rick, and now you too, of course."

I had learned that Sharon and her husband Rick occupied the detached garage apartment in the sprawling backyard. Rick served as the one-man maintenance crew since retiring a few years earlier. Sharon had inherited the property from her aunt and subsequently set out to use it to help women in need.

"Want to grab bowls from that first cabinet to your left?" Sharon motioned with her head as she took the lid off the steaming oatmeal.

"I'm loving our new babysitter already," Rae said. "Less for me to do." She set her coffee cup down on the table as if she were about to take her seat.

"You wish!" Sharon said. "We still need the flatware set."
Rae sighed as she moved to get the utensils. "You're kill-ing me. You and that boy of mine. I can barely function!"

"What a sob story!" Sharon's smile belied her words, and I couldn't help laughing at the good-natured banter.

When the other clients filed into the kitchen, I smiled and nodded, standing back a bit awkwardly until everyone claimed their seats. One young mom came in holding a baby on her hip.

Mentally, I rehearsed the names of those I'd met yester-day. Nicki with baby girl Alanna. Kiya, shy and quiet, expect-ing twins. Judith, also pregnant, who had met me at the door with Rae and baby Melvin. And I had yet to meet Serena who had been kept overnight at the hospital for observation.

"She's adorable," I commented to Nicki, waving at the baby girl. She must have been about five months old. "Her name is Alanna, right?"

"Yeah. Thanks," Nicki said, planting a kiss on the child's head. "She's a handful!" She pulled a highchair from a corner and strapped the baby in as I watched, impressed by how she deftly handled the child and the apparatus.

"Elle," Sharon said, "go ahead and take a seat. Anywhere is fine."

The back door flew open, and Rick hurried in. "Sorry I'm late," he said, washing his hands at the sink. "Got caught up with that motor on the gate. It's acting up again. I had to leave it ajar for when Denise gets here, but I should be able to get it going before long." He took a seat at the table of women and nodded to me. "Elle, how was your first night at Mercy House?"

"Pretty great," I replied. "The room is beautiful and I slept soundly."

"Like a baby," Sharon piped in, winking at me. "Now we better eat before some other babies stop sleeping like that. Honey, will you bless the food?" she asked Rick.

Everyone bowed their heads, and Rick prayed. "Heavenly Father, thank you for this beautiful day and for the privilege of living it. Thank you for this food, Lord. May it nourish our bodies so we can serve you better. In your son Jesus' name, I pray. Amen."

Amens were whispered around the table, and the clinking of dishes and serving spoons ensued as each person helped themselves and passed the food. I couldn't help feeling a little nostalgic. Rick's prayer reminded me of my dad. Even though we'd been estranged for a long time, I still missed him. I missed having family. And without Ethan in my life, I had no family at all.

But this would be my family now. I looked around the table at the girls and Sharon and Rick. Rae had made some wisecrack that set everyone laughing, and I smiled, hoping it wouldn't be long before they accepted me as one of them.

After breakfast, Rick returned to his work outside, and as we were cleaning up, the sound of no-nonsense heels clicking down the long hallway signaled Denise's arrival.

She paused at the kitchen door and nodded to me, before greeting the group as one. "Ladies."

Geesh! This woman's demeanor was like a late winter freeze snuffing out a beautiful spring day.

"Denise," I nodded back, lifting my chin confidently.

I refused to let her throw me off today. This was my place. Mercy House. I wiped the last plate dry and placed it on the shelf. Then, with a sureness in my step—and even a twinge of excitement to get started, I followed Denise to her—and now also my—office.

* * * * *

The rest of the day passed quickly. Denise and Sharon went over the litany of routines and processes while I listened intently and asked questions. Determined to learn quickly, I took detailed notes on everything, including the training the girls received. Parenting classes, nutrition basics, finance management, emotional and psychiatric counseling, Bible studies, prayer meetings. The list seemed endless, and I wondered how they had time for the career training required, which meant working toward their GEDs or taking online college or vocational courses. Not to mention their doctor appointments and household duties. Over the course of the program, ideally by the time the baby was three months old, the client would find daycare and a steady job. That was the transition phase to their graduation, when they would receive help finding safe, affordable housing. And then, by the time the child was five to seven months old, they would move on from Mercy House, after having been here about a year. It made so much sense, I wondered why there weren't thousands of Mercy Houses. Of course, I knew it required a strong fundraising base, but it made me all the more comfortable with the other part of my role, which would be assisting Sharon with her speaking engagements to raise awareness and funds.

Just before lunch, Sharon stepped out to allow Denise time to catch up on emails and me time to get my desk sorted. My mind was spinning with ideas on how to grow the fundraising base. I jotted a few notes on my laptop and glanced over at Denise. Her stiff torso leaned forward, fingers attacking the keyboard with ferocity, her mouth set in a grim line.

Was it just purposeful intent that colored her whole disposition? Or was it about me? Was I a threat to her somehow? I couldn't imagine why. Perhaps funding played into it? Maybe she feared hiring me would strain the budget and threaten her own job.

At the risk of distracting her from her work, I thought maybe I could make some inroads by sharing the fundraising ideas that whirled in my mind. "Have you thought about using emotional appeal to raise funds for Mercy House?" I began tentatively.

Denise looked up from her monitor, and I took it as a cue to let my enthusiasm run.

"I would love to learn more about the clients. And I bet others would too. Maybe we could promote Mercy House through their stories, you know? If we could get them to share their stories in video, the impact could be massive."

I watched with a sinking feeling as her left eyebrow arched and her full lips pursed before she tilted her chin in superiority.

"I see you still aren't grasping the critical importance of security here. Can't you understand how that could endanger the lives of all our clients and also our staff? What would happen if a perpetrator connected to one of our women were to watch such a video and find out about Mercy House? I suggest you stick to what you were hired for—taking care of the household functions and transportation." She turned back to her computer as if to show me the subject was closed.

My first reaction was to kick myself for suggesting the personal stories. I should have thought of the danger. But then I remembered the "Not today" sentiment that got me out of bed.

Allowing indignation to rise, I considered how to respond. *I do understand the importance of the clients' safety, and I can find a way to make anonymous videos . . .* Or, *It's also critical to promote the mission of Mercy House. Not only could these women lose a safe haven, you could lose your job.* And then I would add, *Good thing you're not in charge of promoting it or Mercy House would be no more . . . No Mercy.* And, *If you were in charge of everything, it would have to be called House of No Mercy . . .*

My inner tirade concluded with that last thought. Ridiculous. I knew I was being petty. But I wouldn't let Denise derail me again.

Whatever the issue was, it was her problem, not mine. I took a deep breath and said nothing. Instead, I turned back to my computer and added to my notes: *Don't reveal identities.*

I sure knew how to do that. I was an expert at hiding the truth. Not really lying, I justified. Just wisely holding back. From the time I was a young girl, hiding my family issues with "Mom's got a migraine." To my college years, refusing to claim my Christian upbringing and laughing along with the others at "those crazies." Even to Ethan, not allowing him into my grief, but instead seething with anger at his ability to let it go and even more so at his attempts to pull me from it.

Concealing my true identity was the poison that almost killed me. It left me all alone. How well I knew it.

And how ironic that in coming to Mercy House to rediscover my true self, I was only succumbing to the same voices. *Keep quiet, Elle. Don't let others see your weakness. Don't risk them taking advantage of your vulnerability. You can't trust anyone. Don't let them in.*

Chapter 5

As the days rolled by, the household routines became more familiar. I threw myself wholeheartedly into the work of coordinating the clients' schedules, transporting them to appointments and classes, and managing the household logistics. Their varying appointments tested my organizational skills, but I thrived on the work, feeling happier and healthier than I had in months. It seemed at last the past was the past. Only in the quiet moments did the old feelings raise their ugly heads, and so I stayed occupied as much as possible. Even being around the babies was fine. Since the objective was to promote the clients' self-sufficiency, I was not required to help with them and remained unaffected for the most part—except where Melvin was concerned. Each time I saw him nestled in Rae's arms, my throat knotted up, and I had to look away.

Sharon regularly affirmed the importance of my position and how well I was doing. In fact, she suggested that after I settled in more, she could use my help with blogs that shared the purpose of Mercy House, as well as email campaigns to increase donations to the ministry. I didn't mention the video idea again.

I now recognized the faces that came regularly to meet with the girls. Debbie for mentoring. Kathy for counseling sessions. And the most unforgettable personality, Miss Susie, for a weekly prayer meeting.

Miss Susie came faithfully every Wednesday to pray with the girls in a group setting. A short, round lady in her early sixties, her mousy gray ringlets formed a halo of frizz that made her seem almost angelic, and her laughter, which came often, sounded like the peal of church bells. Her cheerful nature and sweet innocence seemed almost an oxymoron to the wounded and hardened souls that made up Mercy House.

Sweet, but naive.

At least, when she talked about prayer, that's the impression that came to my jaded mind. Her bubbly personality engaged me often, even though I tried to steer clear of her prayer meeting. Coming or going, Miss Susie always made a point to stop by the office and share some word of encouragement or sweet thought. Each time, she asked if she could pray for me. I always assured her there was no need. I appreciated her kindness, but honestly I found it a bit stifling. Strangely, though, the clients hung on her every word. Rae described her to me as a bucket of joy splashing onto everyone she met. And these girls stood close, eager to be splashed on by Miss Susie.

One day, when Miss Susie stopped by after the prayer meeting, Sharon was in the office with me going over her travel schedule.

"Anything I can pray about for you ladies?" Miss Susie

asked in her southern drawl.

I was about to decline politely, but Sharon quickly answered, "I never say no to prayer. I wouldn't be able to do what I do without the faithful prayer support I get from our prayer team."

Sharon's statement surprised me. She wasn't one to patronize, but surely it was exaggerated. I was even more surprised when Miss Susie grasped Sharon's hands and started praying right there. Bowing my head awkwardly, my thoughts warred with what to do. It wasn't like I should continue putting the engagements into Sharon's calendar. And I wasn't about to join them. So I sat still at my desk while the two ladies prayed, Miss Susie's voice becoming loud and fiery at times, and Sharon adding in "Yes, Lord," and "I agree in Jesus' name." I had been around prayer before, but usually they were poetic and carefully edited or a general dinner table blessing like Rick gave. This was like nothing I had experienced before. Weird. Yep, definitely will avoid the prayer group.

Miss Susie went on for what felt like ten minutes, and then Sharon prayed, thanking God for Miss Susie and for me and for all he was doing through the ministry of Mercy House. She didn't pray as loud and forcefully as Miss Susie, but there was an authenticity and vulnerability I admired.

When Miss Susie left, Sharon said, "Wow. I love it when God refreshes me like that. I feel invigorated to go on stronger."

"You know," I offered hesitantly, feeling the need to help Sharon see herself the way I saw her, "I think you're pretty strong already. You mentioned not being able to do what you do without the help of the prayer team, but I think you don't give yourself enough credit."

Sharon waved off the compliment, but I pressed on. I could understand someone like me not seeing my self-worth, but here was a lady who had literally saved hundreds of lives, probably more when you counted the thousands influenced by her speaking engagements and blogs. "Really, Sharon, you are an amazing person. You have so much to be proud of. You started this organization from nothing and have changed so many lives."

"God did." Sharon interrupted me abruptly. "I understand what you're trying to say, and I really do appreciate it. You are very sweet. And you are right that it is good to look back and take stock of how far we've come. But it wasn't me, Elle. It never has been." She took her seat back beside me at the computer. "I know it sounds self-deprecating, but that's not how I feel. I feel very honored that God chose to use me." She sighed, obviously struggling to help me understand what she was trying to say. "Oh, Elle, there is nothing special about me. I'm just an ordinary girl . . . no particular talent or striving for success, just a girl who said, 'Yes, Lord,' and made myself available to carry out His work."

She gave me that classic Sharon smile and suggested we get back to work. I complied, but tucked that into my heart to chew on later. Her reasons for Mercy House were so far from my reasons. I wanted an escape, a feeling of importance, and yes, even the admiration of others. Most of all, I wanted to make a truce with God. An 'I'll scratch your back if you scratch mine' kind of idea.

Did I really think I could strike a bargain with God? How far I was from having a heart like this dear woman!

Lord, help me.

As soon as the words flitted through my mind, I realized that was a prayer and almost laughed out loud. Oh, the wily influence of Miss Susie!

Chapter 6

"Hey, wanna take me grocery shopping with you?" Rae bounced up beside me as I put the finishing touches on the large chore chart I had created.

"Sure . . . ?" My voice dragged the answer into a question, as I turned to look at her. "Do you have some ulterior motive or do you just like monotonous chores like grocery shopping? If the latter, I could add your name in several places on this chart."

Rae had become a regular sidekick, offering help and insight as I learned the routines. Her sense of humor matched my own and she seemed to like having me around.

She gave me an appropriate eye roll. "Of course I love monotony. Can't you tell by the number of diapers I change in a day? No, seriously, I just thought you could use the help, and I could definitely use a break from this place."

"What do you mean 'a break from this place'? Wasn't the pediatrician and counseling appointment and Wednesday night finance class enough for you the last couple of days?"

Between all the clients, I was fairly worn out from driving them to appointments and classes. I would have loved to let someone else do the shopping for the household, but that responsibility was mine. And, I had to admit I would enjoy it more with Rae's company.

"C'mon, Elle, you know you need me. Who's going to show you which pastries are the key to Denise's heart? And besides, we can order one of those lattes you've been missing."

"Your people-reading skills are masterful. I'm impressed by how quickly you've figured out what motivates me. Yes, you can come."

"Yes!" Rae said, clenching her fist in a quick gesture. "Will two this afternoon work? I'll see if Judith can watch Melvin for me while he's napping."

I laughed. "Yes, that will work."

* * * * * * *

Like clockwork, Rae appeared at my side as I sat in front of my computer, jingling keys in my ear.

"Dingalingaling! This is your alarm sounding. It's two o'clock."

"Wow! How come you're not this punctual for breakfast?" I looked up from the spreadsheet I was creating to help keep track of the many moving parts of each client's schedule.

"Because I finally have a sleeping infant and you know he can smell me leaving. C'mon, we gotta move quick!"

I laughed and took the keys from her as I got up. Denise would be furious if she saw Rae with the keys to the van. Clients weren't supposed to have access to them. I wished Denise wasn't a constant concern. Buying her favorite pastries might not be a bad idea. I wasn't above bribery if it could sweeten her attitude a little.

Rae was already out the door, obviously anxious for the break from her sleeping infant. I grabbed my purse and hurried after her. It felt like we were sneaking away for some grand adventure instead of going to the grocery store.

Climbing into the white fifteen-passenger van, I took my time adjusting the seat and mirrors as Rae fiddled with the radio. I wasn't exactly comfortable driving the monstrous vehicle, but I had been getting plenty of practice. As soon as I eased onto the paved road, Rae blasted the tunes. Pink was playing and she turned it up louder, moving her body to the beat as much as the seatbelt would allow her to. "Partaaay time!!!!" she shouted.

I laughed. Rae had certainly made me feel comfortable at Mercy House. I had barely been here two weeks, yet I was already finding my groove, thanks to her. I glanced at her making silly dance moves constrained by the seatbelt. She had changed from her normal attire of a baggy T-shirt and sweatpants into a red and black flannel shirt and jeans. Her short, sleek hair was braided into two pigtails that barely touched each shoulder, and a tasseled beanie that topped her head bobbed to the rhythm of the music. Such a cute beanie. I needed to pull out my hat stock. If Rae could make a beanie work here in April, I could certainly do hats again, too.

I envied the comfortable-in-her-own-skin vibe she had going—something I had not yet achieved. It seemed like all my life I had tried to be someone else, and as a result, here I was still trying to figure out who exactly was the real Eleanor Anders.

Funny, now I'm just wishing I can be as comfortable as Rae. This pattern had to stop! I needed to learn to do me. For starters, I liked music. And I could dance. Smiling broadly, I let my body begin moving to the music.

"Yeah!" Rae said, nodding her head in approval.

I pounded out the rhythm on the steering wheel, laughing as I let myself enjoy the music.

We were still bobbing and weaving in our seats as I pulled the white monster into the store parking lot. I drove all the way to the back of the lot to avoid parking next to another car.

"You've got to be kidding me," Rae said, as I slammed the shift stick into park and turned off the ignition. "Is this a not-so-subtle hint that I still have baby fat to lose? It's a half-mile hike to the front door."

"Stop your whining," I said, remembering Sharon's teasing response to Rae's sarcasm. "You're not the one having to park this beast. And the walk will be good for us."

Once inside, I grabbed the cart while Rae offered to go get our lattes from the store cafe.

"Skinny vanilla latte double shot," Rae repeated to herself as she walked away with my order.

I opened the grocery list on my phone and headed for

the produce. I'd always detested grocery store shopping. Ethan had spoiled me by doing that chore when we were together. It wasn't so easy in Boston without a car. He got most of our groceries from DeLuca's Market, but faithfully every week, he went to the farmer's market for fresh produce and novelty baked goods. Occasionally, I would go with him and we would make a date of it, perusing Quincy Market and getting lunch at Fanueill Hall. Since grocery shopping was part of my job now, maybe I would follow Ethan's example and make the effort to go to a farmer's market each week. And since it was much better with company, I could plan to take one of the girls with me as their schedules allowed.

I was halfway through my list when Rae finally returned with my latte.

"That took a while," I said.

"Well, you know, it's that time of day when everyone is looking for a java jolt." Rae sipped her latte and turned to look over the cereals.

"I was waiting to go to the baked goods. I'm absolutely taking you up on the offer to find the key to Denise's heart. It may mean life or death for my career here."

"Aw, you can't take Denise too seriously. She takes herself too seriously. She's really a chocolate lava cake. You just gotta push hard enough to get through that crusty layer and you'll find that her gooey heart really is pretty sweet."

"I don't know," I said hesitantly, pushing the cart as Rae walked beside me. "She's my boss. I can't exactly push back on her and expect to keep my job. She was ready to get rid of me the first day."

"Mark my words: she's a lot of bluff on the outside."

"Oh, I'm forgetting you're the master people-reader," I said. "What insight can you give me on the girls? I mean clients."

Rae plucked a bag of pretzels off the shelf and dropped it into the cart. "Well, Nicki, she's a good apple. Had a hard life on the streets. She was trafficked before she got to Mercy House. A wounded soul, and sometimes that comes out as cat claws, but don't take it personally."

I shook my head. It was awful imagining the lives these women had lived. I sighed and looked at my list, trying to multi-task as Rae continued.

"Yeah, one time she got into it with Denise, and it was not pretty. But guess what? She's still here. See, told ya, Denise is a real softy when you get to know her."

Rae bagged some apples as I looked over the avocados, trying to find some that weren't rock-hard.

"Now, Serena, she's a case," Rae said, as I began pushing the cart again. "There's always something up with that girl. Can you say 'hypochondriac'?"

"What?" I responded incredulously. "She went to the hospital and was put on bedrest. There must be something wrong with her."

"Wrong like bribing the doctor to get her out of work."

"Come on. That's pretty far fetched."

"Okay, well, that may be extreme, but I'm telling you that

girl is a lot healthier than she lets on."

"Alright, well, what about Judith? Putting her baby up for adoption? I don't understand how that's a consideration when you're at a place that is basically setting you up for success as a mom. Who gives up their baby by choice?"

"Hey," Rae said, stopping short to face me. "You don't know anything about her situation."

I stopped the cart, realizing how judgmental I sounded. How judgmental I was.

"It actually takes guts to admit that your baby would have a better life without you." Rae fell silent for a moment, then continued, "And it takes love to go through with it. Judith loves her child enough that she's willing to give him up even though it means her arms will ache for him the rest of her life."

I swallowed hard. I knew that ache, but it hadn't come through self-sacrifice. I hoped Judith could handle it better than I did.

"You're right." I nodded, unsure what else to say. I felt two inches tall. Why had I allowed my thoughts to fly unfiltered?

"Let's go get those pastries," Rae said, turning toward the bakery. "Melvin's going to be looking for me soon."

Chapter 7

Late one afternoon in early May, I sat at my desk clicking through documents when the doorbell rang.

"Want me to get that?" Rae yelled down the hallway.

"Very funny." I got up from my desk and made my way to the door when Denise came striding past me.

"I will get the door," Denise said. "I'm expecting CPS with a new client."

I hung back as she opened the door and greeted the caseworker. Beside her stood a young woman staring off into the distance, as if she'd rather be anywhere but on the front porch of Mercy House. A large T-shirt dress draped her heavy-set frame, and worn, dingy slippers hinted that they could be her only shoes. A plastic garbage bag, with what I assumed were her belongings, was slung over her shoulder.

The caseworker introduced her as Brilanna, and I smiled warmly, trying to emulate the same warmth Sharon had greeted me with on my first day. But Brilanna didn't even look my way. The stench of body odor filled my nostrils as she passed by. Discreetly, I covered my nose and followed as Denise led the way down the hall.

Sharon and Rick were out of the country on speaking engagements, so we used her office, which luckily was large enough to dissipate the foul odor.

Brilanna slumped back in her chair, silent and sullen, even bored maybe? I tried to concentrate on the details the caseworker rattled off, making notes on my Mac as she spoke. Nineteen years old, four months pregnant, living on the streets, with a fifteen-month-old child. CPS had already taken the toddler to foster care. Baby daddy was recently arrested on charges of burglary and aggravated assault.

My stomach churned as my fingers clicked across the keyboard. I focused on the screen, grateful to conceal the judgment forming in my mind. Hearing about hardened backgrounds was still a very new facet of the job, and the details made me want to vomit.

After the caseworker finished, Denise walked her out, leaving me to question Brilanna in order to apply for Medicaid she would need for doctor appointments. The girl appeared annoyed, answering my questions with sighs and eye rolls, never once looking me in the eye. I wanted to shake her and tell her how thankful she should be that people like us care enough to help her. Instead, I quickly entered the details and escorted her to the storage closet where we kept donated supplies, including clean clothes and presentable shoes.

By the time I had finished my duties of settling Brilanna in her room, my nerves felt jagged and raw like a bandage ripped from a wound much too soon. Hurrying down the hall to my own room, I closed the door behind me and slid to a heap on the floor. *Ungrateful. Undeserving.* The words came unbidden to my thoughts, followed by hot tears that sprung to my eyes, threatening to spill over.

I clutched my stomach, remembering the life that had been there.

Why?? Why do these girls who don't even want a child and can't care for them have not one but two babies, while mine is taken from me?? It's not right. It's not fair.

Yet, right after the words formed in my mind, I realized that, for those first awful weeks, I had been that ungrateful, undeserving girl. Scared. Unprepared. Ashamed that I let this happen. I choked back the sobs that formed in my throat and buried my head in my knees to muffle the sounds that came like deep moans from within.

I can't, God. I can't handle this.

A tap at the door shocked me into silence, and I kept my face buried against my knees as I heard the door creak open.

"Elle?"

It was Rae.

"You okay?"

"Yeah," I answered, carefully controlling my voice. "Just a headache."

It wasn't a lie. The sinus pressure from unshed tears made my head feel like it would explode.

"Can I get you anything?"

"No." I hoped she would leave quickly. "Thanks."

Softly, the door clicked shut and I breathed out a shaky sigh as pent-up tears seeped down my face.

* * * * * * *

I tried to erase the bias I felt toward Brilanna, remembering Sharon's warning from my first conversation with her. "Real life is messy." But there was no getting around the decidedly negative vibe she brought to the once tranquil Mercy House. Everyone was on edge around her. Even the babies seemed more fussy than usual.

Kiya, the most easy-going of our clients, was the one who had to share a room with her. It didn't seem fair, but I think Denise secretly hoped that her quiet, gentle spirit would rub off on Brilanna. I know I did.

Honestly, the girl was obstinate, ungrateful, apathetic, and even undermining—to the point that even our patient and compassionate counselor, Kathy, had discontinued sessions with her.

"A key component of this counseling process is that the client must be willing," Kathy told me and Denise when she stopped by the office to cancel the next session. "Brilanna is certainly not willing, and until that happens, I'm afraid she's only wasting my time. I told her to let me know when she's serious about finding freedom, but until then, I can't help her. I'm sorry."

It didn't help that Sharon and Rick were still abroad on

their tour of speaking engagements. I was anxious to see how Sharon would handle Brilanna's personality. Brilanna regularly conflicted with someone, primarily around adhering to tasks and schedules. Most had learned to just let her be, but Nikki refused to let her slack off, which often turned into a shouting match. And that's usually when Denise got involved. Our no-nonsense director had called her into a private meeting four times in the two weeks she'd been here, plus she had me book a consultation in Sharon's calendar. Likely, it was to determine ultimatums, but I wasn't so sure Brilanna could last here until Sharon returned. I really doubted it when Nikki accused her of trying to hurt her daughter.

"She covered her head with a blanket while she was sleeping!" Nikki's face was hot with anger as she reported this to Denise when we all gathered in the living room for our daily meeting. I remembered what Rae had said about Nikki's cat-claw personality that showed itself every so often, but this was more like the claws of a mama bear.

"I ain't done nothin' like that," Brilanna retorted.

"I saw you on the video monitor!" Nikki's voice boomed, out of control with anger.

"You calling me a liar?"

"Yes, I am. You're a liar and a monster!"

Brilanna flinched. She started to respond but then clenched her teeth. "I was just trying to help her. I only wanted her to be warm."

"Stay away from my daughter! If you so much as get near

her again, you won't live to regret it."

"Nikki!" Denise's commanding voice broke in.

Brilanna looked almost ready to cry.

"One of us has to leave," Nikki said, the fury still radiating from her. "If you don't get rid of her, I'm taking my daughter and leaving now."

Miss Susie had slipped in quietly for prayer group while we were preoccupied with the situation. She came forward and gently put her arm around Nikki. "Honey, let's go pray."

The tough-girl exterior hesitated like a hologram losing connection. She shook her head. "Miss Susie, I don't think I can."

"This is *why* we pray, darlin'. God can take care of your sweet little angel, and He will give you the wisdom on how to handle this."

"Brilanna, you come with me," Denise said curtly. "We are going to have a heart-to-heart about your boundaries here."

Brilanna's face that moments ago looked like it could melt into tears hardened back into steel.

Chapter 8

Things calmed down a little after the eruption of emotion between Nikki and Brilanna. Apparently Miss Susie had worked her magic, and Nikki was willing to give Brilanna another chance. A new sense of compassion toward her developed in me as well. The crack in her steeled exterior helped me see she was just as human as the rest of us—a wounded soul in need of love. But she certainly didn't make it easy. Rae dubbed her Bad-Attitude Bri, and called her Babs for short, even to her face. Somehow Rae could get away with that, and it seemed Brilanna even warmed up to her a bit because of it.

In Sharon's absence, a respite worker named Carolyn was staying at the house to help manage evening activities after Denise left. A grandmotherly type, she mainly sat in a rocker with a baby on her lap and a good-natured smile on her face, happily letting everyone do as they pleased.

The girls had picked up on her relaxed vibe pretty quickly, so it was really down to me to enforce the evening rules. I felt almost like Denise, to the point that the girls—okay, Rae—had begun calling me a fun-sucker.

To prove her wrong and to shake off the damper Brilanna

brought to the house, I decided to throw a slumber party on Friday night. The inspiration hit when a donor brought dozens of bottles of nail polish, lotions, and facial masks for the clients to enjoy. A good old-fashioned slumber party would be a great way to let the girls just be girls for a night, and I hoped it could be a bonding experience.

In my weekly shopping, I picked up some frozen pizzas, popcorn, and four bags of Rae's favorite Trollies to add to the fun. I let the girls in on the surprise, but no one told Denise. As a result, they were antsy with anticipation when Denise ended up staying late Friday evening, supposedly concerned about how things would go over the weekend. This would be the trial run for me 'in charge' of the household, although Denise and Sharon both trusted Carolyn implicitly. Guaranteed, Denise herself would be staying the weekend if that weren't the case. And as the minutes dragged by, we all began to wonder.

Finally, she said goodbye. Serena, 'conveniently' no longer on bedrest, stood watch at the window, giving us a play-by-play.

"Almost there . . . closer . . . Okay, she's in the car!" Pause. "Whatchu doing, lady? Clipping your toenails??" A longer pause with a groan, then, "Finally! She's backing up. Now going forward. She's at the gate! Gate opening . . . Going through . . . Closing . . ." Her voice trailed upward, following the snail-like movement of the gate. "Alright! Hit it, Judith!" She spun around and pointed to Judith who stood ready at the stereo, finger poised on the play button.

The tune *Cheap Thrills* by Sia blasted from the speakers,

and it seemed the entire house began pulsating with the beat. Carolyn grinned broadly as Nikki snatched baby Alanna from her lap and joined the others as they danced their way to the family room. I laughed at the scene unfolding before me, shaking my head as I watched three pregnant women moving their big baby bumps to the rhythm with two other ladies holding babies on their hips as they danced.

An unlikely sisterhood, I thought, but motherhood has a way of doing that. The fierce strength of motherly love unites women of every color and culture—and that is true no matter the child's age, stage, status . . . or presence. I turned away with a tinge of sadness and pre-heated the oven to 425.

From the corner of my eye, I saw that Brilanna had sidled up next to the kitchen counter and perched on a stool, drawn into the open kitchen and family room by the pulsating music. Rae noticed her at the same time and yelled, "Come on in, Babs! The music feels great!"

'Babs' came as close to smiling as I'd seen yet, but waved away the invitation.

"What?" Rae persisted. "You don't have the moves like we do?"

That elicited a snicker from her. "Nah, I just don't wanna show you up."

"Challenge taken!" Rae shouted back. "Get that booty out here!"

To my wide-eyed amazement, Babs pitched off her new fluffy turquoise slippers and bumped her way onto the makeshift dance floor as Rae and the others cheered their approval.

The tone was set for the evening, and I felt almost like I was in a sorority again—but this group of girls was a cultural world away from those I'd known in college. With limited options for movies, I paired my computer to the TV and streamed *Breakfast at Tiffany's*, ignoring the cries for a thriller. We munched popcorn and Trollies amidst a running commentary of the pros and cons of a life like Audrey Hepburn's.

"You know she nearly starved to death as a teenager in the Netherlands during World War 2," I said, biting into a colorful gummy worm. As Rae had predicted, I had become hooked on the sugar-coated sour candies, so much so that I didn't even feel guilty about eating them while discussing Hepburn's plight. "After her acting career, she devoted her life's work to the organization that had helped her and her family survive those years."

"No way," Nikki said. "I never knew that about her. That's really cool."

"Yeah, she lived with her sons in Switzerland, but she did hardened runs into war torn areas in Africa," I said, reaching for another Trolli. "A pretty amazing woman—a real soldier in humanitarian efforts."

Judith eased herself onto the floor, waiting her turn for Nikki to braid her hair. "How do you know so much about her?" she asked.

"I've always loved all things Audrey—who doesn't love her?" I said, remembering my mom who adored this movie. We only watched it when Dad wasn't home. It's a special movie just for us girls, Mom would say. But I knew it was because Dad didn't approve of the smoking and 'wild living' it portrayed. Somehow, he never saw the humanity in it. The heart of a girl searching for identity.

When Mom was healthy and I was just a little girl, she took me on a trip to New York, just the two of us. We bought croissants and ate them outside the Tiffany's store on Fifth Avenue, just like Holly Golightly in the movie. The memory always brought a warm feeling in my chest. She and I had talked about it often. A fun, shared memory. After she died, I guess I tried to keep something about her close by carrying on the love for Audrey.

"On my backpacking travels during college, I saw her home in Switzerland and a museum about her in that town."

"Switzerland?" Serena said, obviously impressed. "And I thought all they had was a little miss who makes yummy hot chocolate packets."

"Switzerland is the most beautiful place I've ever seen," I said, thinking back to the lush green hills covered in white flowers with towering snow-capped Alps behind them.

"I wish I could travel the world!" Judith said. "I've never been farther than Louisiana. Where else did you go?"

"All around Europe in that one trip," I said, reminiscing about the fun time Ethan and I had together the summer after our sophomore year.

We had gone with a group of friends, but Ethan and I ended up doing our own thing for the most part. That was when

I knew we were falling in love. We found all sorts of hole-in-the-wall places and oddities that we thought were hilarious.

I laughed out loud, remembering them. "There was this one museum in Sweden called the disgusting food museum—it was awful!" I said, laughing. "They had maggot-infested cheese and fermented fish. The smells were horrible! They even had a tasting bar to try things, complete with barf bags which Ethan had to use!" I stopped short, realizing I had said his name aloud for the first time in months.

"Ethan?" Nikki said, dragging out both syllables dramatically. "Oo-la-la! Who's Ethan?"

I sobered quickly, refusing to go there with the girls. "Let's suffice it to say, we all have histories," I said, trying to sound chipper. Pretending not to notice the side-eyed glances between them, I stood up and resumed my leadership role. "How about you all put these babies to bed? And get your faces washed and PJ's on so we can start our pampering time."

After the babies were fed and put down for the night with Carolyn's help, we all returned to the living room with hair covered or pulled back in tight bands. The girls swarmed the polish and face masks and grabbed their selections. I chose mine last, and soon our faces were covered with shiny paper masks as we settled down to paint each other's toes. Babs had chosen a green avocado mask, but refused the toe painting no matter how much she was cajoled by the others. Instead, she tucked her calloused feet back into the turquoise slippers, safely away from any polish.

Within minutes, we could feel the cleansing effects of the masks as they tightened to our faces making it difficult to speak and even harder to smile. The conversation had turned to boyfriends and baby daddies. I couldn't blame them for wanting to make a life with the father of their child, but sadly most of them were here because the father was not a good person to be involved with.

Kiya, always quiet and reserved, spoke up. "I think every child should have the opportunity to know their father if they can. I want my twins to have a good relationship with their dad because, in spite of all his faults, he's a part of them. I'm hoping he will be with me for the birth."

"I had Jesse with me when Melvin was born," Rae said. "It seemed right that he was there to experience the birth. He even got to cut the cord."

"Not every man deserves to be part of that," Babs muttered, barely loud enough for us to hear. As all eyes turned toward her, she responded with a look of defiance. "You think any man can be a father just because he has the right parts?"

"Nobody is saying that," Nikki replied.

"But you think you can have a happy family if the baby daddy comes along, right?" Babs said, shaking her head as her personality came alive with exaggerated gestures. "Then everything will be perfect. Lemme tell you, that even with a baby daddy who supposedly loves you and his kids, if he a fool, ain't no taking the fool outta the man. He'll drag you and your kids through the junk he goin' through."

"Not everyone has a baby daddy like that," Judith offered diplomatically.

"You think you here because you got a Prince Charming?" Babs responded.

"You don't know anything about any of our situations," Nikki interjected.

"And you don't know the half of what people in this world are like. I seen the worst of the worst when I was living on the streets."

I didn't like where this conversation was going, but my face had stiffened under my mask, so I remained mute.

"Oh, you're the only one who's had a hard life?" Nikki jumped to her feet. "You come in here wearing a chip on your shoulder like you're somehow different than the rest of us because you've had it tough?"

"All I'm sayin' is some come from a place of priv'lege and will never know what the real world is like."

Were her words pointed at me? A place of privilege. Probably the only college graduate in the room. From a middle-class family, married into upper middle-class even.

"Privilege?" Nikki said. "You mean like the privilege of being here at Mercy House? Let me tell you every one of us has come out of the gutter by the grace of God. Some of us choose to forgive and let go of the past."

Her charcoal-masked face squared off with Babs's avocado green one as Babs stood to her feet.

I could feel the anger simmering in the room, oddly

juxtaposed to the almost comical scene unfolding. I wondered if I should stop it, but my mouth remained clamped down as I absorbed Nikki's words.

"Forgive?? Are you crazy enough to think that everything can just be forgiven and forgotten? You have no idea what I been through. My mama left me to fend for myself when I was just fourteen. I been living on the streets ever since. Dragged through hell by my baby daddy. Stuff I seen can't ever be forgotten. Includin' watchin' my baby scream as cops pulled him from my arms." Babs's voice cracked. But she recovered quickly and shouted, "So don't you talk to me about forgivin' and forgettin'!"

Babs grabbed at her face, the expressive comment apparently causing discomfort.

"You think being held against your will and forced to sleep with dirty old men is easy to forgive?" Nikki boomed.

I froze, wide-eyed, knowing I should intervene, but not sure what to do. Were they really going to fight?

Babs ripped off her green mask as if she were pulling off boxing gloves. But what followed was a pained yelp and a string of expletives.

Nikki's anger dissolved into laughter, and I held my breath, still hoping a physical altercation would not ensue. But then she grabbed her own face, obviously in pain from laughing against the tight mask.

To my relief, Babs smiled and rubbed her face. "Dang, that hurt."

But as I now realized, that was the least of the hurt

she'd endured. Same with Nikki and the others. The night had opened my eyes to the depravity of the worlds they came from. So different from my own.

They assumed I led a charmed life. But no one knew the truth of the depths I'd traveled—not at the hands of others, but my own. And no one could know, because I refused to dredge up the past. I wanted to be free of it like Nikki said, but I knew I hadn't forgiven and let go. How could I? I had a choke hold on it. And if I let go, surely it would rise up and crush me once again.

Chapter 9

Despite the heated debate between Nikki and Babs, the slumber party proved to be a bigger success than I had imagined, and I was happy to no longer be known as the funsucker. When Denise returned for work on Monday morning, the camaraderie in our household was noted even by the real funsucker herself.

"I can see you are bonding with the clients," Denise said during our afternoon meeting. "I want to warn you not to let your emotions get involved here, Elle. This place is a revolving door, and the emotional attachments can be messy. These clients need support, guidance, and stability, not friendship."

I listened quietly, but I wanted to shout that her biggest problem was just that. Her refusal to make emotional connections made the house feel like a sterile clinic under her guidance. It was one thing to maintain professional relationships in a business setting, but this was a home. I determined not to take her advice, well-intended or not.

The slumber party had done great things for the girls' happiness, which, in my opinion, could only improve things. Despite the near fist-fight, a rawness was revealed that helped me empathize with each of the clients in a new way—even Babs. I understood the pain of her loss. The funny thing about loss is that although its circumstances are often so different, the lingering grief can feel the same. And yet, its effect can take so many forms. Sometimes it can create a knowing, even bonding experience. But in other cases, like with me and Ethan, it could rip you apart.

Even though Babs remained mostly moody and sullen, she showed moments of letting her guard down. It took the edge off things just knowing that she might one day become part of the sisterhood. By the time Sharon and Rick returned home later that week, she had settled into a cadence that was all her own. In the evenings, under my watch, she was mostly relaxed and would sometimes enter into conversation with the other girls, though she rarely said much. By day, however, surliness practically oozed from her pores.

True to the character we had come to know, Babs rolled her eyes about going to the prayer group when I knocked on the open bedroom door to tell the clients Miss Susie had arrived. The other girls grabbed their Bibles and headed downstairs to the meeting room, but Babs merely muttered something about not feeling well and rolled over on her bed to face the wall.

I headed back into the office, shaking my head. "I wish there was something we could do to encourage Brilanna to engage in things like the prayer group."

Denise looked at me over her glasses and frowned. "Encourage?" She stood up, and I instantly regretted voicing my thoughts to her. "I've got some encouragement for her."

She marched out the door and I could hear every step as she thudded determinedly up the staircase, probably giving herself shin splints as she went.

Ugh! Why do you do this? Don't you understand this is just going to make her more obstinate? I knew personalities like this— including my teenage self. You push them and they harden further. She would completely undo the progress I had made. *Nobody wants to be pushed. You have to create buy-in.*

But I knew Denise would never listen to my voice of reason, so I simply met her at the door of the meeting room when she returned. Babs trudged behind her, resentment written all over the younger woman's face. Denise swept her arms in an exaggerated motion to show her the way into the room before continuing briskly back to the office.

I sighed deeply and tried to smile for Babs. "Don't worry, the other clients love it, and I'm sure you will too if you just give it a chance."

Hatred seemed to seep out of her pores as she stepped past me.

"Of course she will," Miss Susie said cheerfully, putting an arm around Babs as she guided her into the room. "And, Elle, I bet you'd love it too. Would you like to join us?"

Deer in the headlights moment.

I tried to blink away the surprise as I fumbled for an excuse that wouldn't discourage Babs.

"Yes, join us!" Kiya said. "You'll love it! It's the best hour of the whole week."

I plastered on a smile that didn't quite make it to my eyes. "I don't have a Bible with me," I faltered.

"That's okay, I'll share with you," Nikki offered.

Ugh . . .

I entered the room and sat next to Kiya on the sofa, trying to mask my reluctance.

"I'm so glad we have newcomers!" Miss Susie exclaimed in her Texas twang. "I love getting to explain our format."

I clamped my lips and nodded. I'd been in many prayer groups when I was growing up. Typically, they ended up with one person sharing a sob story. Or worse, turned into a gossip-fest about why we needed to pray for so and so.

"First of all, you should know that normally we don't talk about praying here. We just pray," Miss Susie said, as if she had some listening device tuned to my mental track. "However, I really want y'all to get this," she said, looking at me and Babs. "So, I'm going to take some time to explain it. After that, we will jump right into prayer and just pray our requests. Moms in Prayer is an international organization of women who meet together each week to pray. We pray conversationally, which means we pray just like we are in a conversation, but one that includes the God of the universe!" Her church bell peal of laughter caused a contagious ripple of laughter around our little circle. "We follow a simple four step format to keep us on track. Kiya, can you tell us those four steps?"

"Praise, confession, thanksgiving, and intercession." She

counted off the words as Miss Susie nodded her encouragement.

"Exactly! Each of those is in the Lord's Prayer, you know, and each has a unique purpose. We start with praise, focusing on who God is. Throughout the Scriptures, we see instruction to praise."

My stomach turned with nausea at the realization of what I had stepped into. Praise? As in the singing they do at church?

I had been tolerating church okay so far, but still, the idea nauseated me. Yes, I wanted to connect with God. I wanted to feel him. I wanted to hear him. I wanted some answers. But the whole idea of having to sing our way to get him to answer. I hated that. It seemed so . . . manipulative.

"Now, of course, God doesn't need our praise," Miss Susie said. I tried not to squirm, more convinced than ever that she was hearing my inner thoughts. She leaned in as if she had some amazing secret she was about to divulge to our little circle. "God's people are instructed to praise him for our own benefit. Psalm 8:2 tells us that he ordains the praise of infants and children. From our earliest days, we are innately made to praise God. Why? Verse 2 goes on to say that it is to silence the foe and the avenger. Praise is your weapon."

Miss Susie's eyes grew fierce in a way that indicated there was more to her than sweetness and sunshine. She seemed powerful and a bit intimidating in a way I couldn't quite put my finger on.

"We praise God by declaring who he is," Miss Susie said. "Praise is truth about God declared from your heart—it's not about singing, though it can be done that way, but here we simply speak out that truth."

I breathed a sigh of relief.

"When we speak that truth out loud, it silences the enemy. It also builds our faith, taking our focus off of our own needs and placing them on the one who cares for all our needs. Now, what is the second of the four steps of prayer, Rae?"

"Confession," Rae answered, without a trace of her normal wit or sarcasm tacked on. I smirked, waiting for a sly glance or funny face, but nothing came.

"Yes!" Miss Susie said with such animation that a bystander would have thought Rae won the jackpot. I almost laughed out loud, but stopped myself, noting how serious everyone seemed. I was baffled, watching these hardened-by-life women hang on every word from this grandma talking about God. It was mesmerizing in a way. Consciously, I tried to remove my bias and listen to her open-mindedly. But it sure wasn't easy.

"Confession is critical," Miss Susie said, growing very serious. "We don't want anything to stand between us and God. Sin separates us from God. But 1 John 1:9 tells us that when we confess our sins, God is faithful and just—because Jesus's death paid the debt of sin for us—to forgive us and cleanse us from all unrighteousness. So, during this silent time of confession, ask the Holy Spirit to search your heart. Allow him to bring to mind anything you need to confess. Any wrong attitude, bad thoughts, unforgiveness toward others—whatever it is, admit it to God and ask for his forgiveness."

Nikki glanced over at Babs. "That's choosing to forgive," she said almost under her breath. But Miss Susie caught it.

"You are so right, Nikki," Miss Susie said. "It's natural to think that we have to feel like forgiving someone in order to actually forgive, but the truth is if we confess that unforgiveness to the Lord, he will cleanse our hearts so that we can actually forgive them. He's the one that can help us choose to release others from punishment we think they deserve."

Miss Susie paused and looked around the circle at each one of us, as if she were gathering up her thoughts, and then she launched them at us. "And they might really deserve punishment. Just like we deserved to be separated from God forever because Romans 6:3 says the punishment for sin is death. Yet, God chose to forgive us while we were still sinners. We can do the same for others. In fact, God tells us to do the same for others. There's a teaching in Mark chapter 11 about that. Jesus is talking about prayer. He says that whatever you ask for in prayer, believe that you have received it, and it will be yours, *but*," Miss Susie said, dragging the word out emphatically with her short index finger in the air, "then he adds that when you stand praying, if you hold anything against anyone, forgive them so that your Father in heaven will forgive you."

I stole a glance toward Babs who was sitting next to me. Her expression was stoic, hard.

Chapter 10

Babs's jaw clenched and released. She stared at the floor as Miss Susie continued her teaching. Disgust welled up in me as I suddenly felt protective of this obstinate but hurting girl. How dare Miss Susie push her ideas about forgiveness when she had absolutely no clue what Babs had been through! Clearly, she wasn't a mind reader or she never would ask that of these girls. Or maybe she would, which was just cruel. Denise was just as guilty of cruelty for forcing her into this group way too early. Babs had come so close to opening up when we were relaxed at the slumber party, and now this was sure to set her back.

"Okay, well, I'm talking way too much," Miss Susie said, leaning back in her chair. "We need to get praying! Let me just finish this by saying that thanksgiving is the next step. It differs from praise in that, rather than focusing on who God is, we focus on what He has done for us."

I had a feeling I wouldn't be able to conjure up any thanks. I was not very happy. My mind darted a thousand different ways about how to get both Babs and myself out of this. But Denise . . . Breathe in. One. Two. Three. And out. One. Two. Three.

I willed myself to calm down. What would Sharon do? Obviously, she would have Babs in here. She's the one who approved this group meeting in the first place. So, listen. Focus. My inner voice now sounded like Sharon. Don't try to imagine what will happen next. Just take it moment by moment.

I tuned my ears back to Miss Susie's soliloquy.

"Thanksgiving is another thing that God instructs us to do so that we benefit. It is a key to joy. Don't miss that, ladies." Again, the finger wag.

Deep breath. One. Two . . .

"It is also a faith-builder. When we focus on what he has already done for us, it builds our faith to know we can trust him to take care of the things for which we are about to intercede. Each of these steps builds on the one before it so that we come to the next step—intercession—prepared for battle. Intercession is where we pray for others."

Miss Susie handed Babs and me a "prayer sheet" as she called it. The other girls already had theirs with their Bibles opened. I cringed inside as I looked at the sheet. So formal. So odd. I hadn't prayed out loud since I was a young girl, and I dreaded the awkwardness. I found myself hoping Denise would call me out of the room even if it was to berate me for something I did or didn't do.

No such luck.

Nikki shared her Bible with me as the girls took turns reading the opening Bible passages. Then, Miss Susie launched into prayer.

"Father, thank you for meeting us here today. I praise you for being our God who is with us always, and I thank you for your Word that tells us you will never leave us or forsake us."

Surprisingly, unlike her long-winded explanation, that's all she said.

A few seconds of awkward silence followed before Kiya spoke up. "Yeah, God," she said softly. "You've always been there for me. Even when I never saw you. And even when I did see you but ignored you. Thank you for never giving up wanting to be with me."

Something in my heart softened with her words. I had come to love Ki in my short time at Mercy House. To hear her speak so earnestly with God made me feel not like I was eavesdropping, but like I was being included in an intimate friendship.

All the other girls except Babs spoke up one by one, each with short prayers to God about his nearness or presence. Rae, whom everyone loved for being "real," told God that she was thankful that he had met her at her lowest point. "You're the God who sees and loves. Thank you for seeing me and loving me in spite of the junk I was involved in. You were willing to find me right there and show me the way out."

There were small pauses and I kept trying to think of what to say, but then, thankfully, someone would speak up again. Before I was put on the spot, Miss Susie started on the next step in the prayer sheet.

"Holy Spirit, we invite you to search our hearts," she said.

"Point out anything that we need to confess to you and give us the courage to do it in Jesus' name."

I looked up, thinking the prayer was over, but everyone's eyes were still closed, even Babs.

"Let's just take a few silent moments here to let God bring to mind anything we need to confess," Miss Susie said. I bent forward in my chair, studying my shoes and looking at everyone else's. Rae sat cross-legged on the floor, head bowed. Babs's turquoise fuzzy slippers next to me shifted as she crossed and then recrossed her ankles.

The silence seemed unbearably long, although it was probably only two minutes. Then I heard what sounded like a sob beside me. Then a sniff. Then multiple sniffs in a row. I glanced over at Babs. Her eyes were tightly closed and tears streamed down her face. Anxiously, I looked toward Miss Susie who caught my eye. Her expression was unconcerned, serene even. She shook her head just slightly, indicating I shouldn't interrupt anything.

I clenched and unclenched my hands, trying to relax. This was definitely out of my comfort zone. I refocused on the stitching on my sneakers and painfully endured the prolonged silence punctuated by sniffs from Babs.

By the time we moved on to the thanksgiving step, I had already determined in my mind that I would not be attending again. And that's when Babs spoke up.

In a low, hoarse voice, she said, "Thank you, God, for forgivin' me. And thank you for helping me forgive my mom.

I know she done the best she could."

It was so out of character for this angry, sullen young woman. She hardly ever spoke to anyone, and when she did, she sounded either belligerent or annoyed. Yet, here she was being vulnerable in front of all of us.

Before I could contemplate it, Miss Susie announced that we would be praying for our children during the intercession step. Suddenly that old familiar pang filled the hollow in my chest.

"You can just insert your child's name in the blank spaces of that next verse on your prayer sheet," Miss Susie explained to Babs. "Go ahead," she encouraged gently. "Read the verse."

Babs began tentatively reading the verse written with blank spaces. Her reading level was probably not higher than a ten-year-old's. She read slowly and haltingly, "God promised: I will never leave—" She stopped suddenly as she reached the blank in the sentence. She swiped at the tears rolling down her cheeks and shook her head. "I ain't said his name since they took him away," she said hoarsely.

I looked at Miss Susie for her response. I was ready to lead Babs out of the room. This was torture. But Babs started reading again. "God promises: I will never leave Isaiah nor forsake him. I will be with Isaiah wherever—" She broke down weeping before she could complete the sentence. And Miss Susie picked it up, reading the Bible verse and praying for Isaiah as if this young mom's heart wasn't ripping out of her. Yet with each word Miss Susie spoke, Babs's sobs changed, lessened.

My heart remained in my throat as the other women took turns praying for Babs's child. Their words became muffled as my senses honed in on Babs' sniffles. I should have refused to come to this prayer meeting. *Moms in Prayer?* No one had told me the name. Of course it was for mothers to pray for their children. What were they thinking even inviting me here? All of them knew I had no children. Yet none of them knew I was a mom just like them. A mom who knew the love for a child. A mom who had felt the flutter of life in her womb. A mom who heard the rapid beat of her baby's heart. And then, a mom with empty arms.

My heart began beating in my ears, pounding so loudly that Miss Susie's voice was far away as she turned to me. She said words I couldn't hear, something about who I could pray for—friends, nieces, nephews. I was looking toward her but could only see images of the motionless sonogram. *A missed miscarriage . . . a seventeen-week-old fetus to be extracted by surgery . . . a D&C.* I heard my desperate pleas from the sterile hospital bed, begging the nurse to check one more time for a heartbeat before the anesthesia put me to sleep. And then I saw her. The little girl I had imagined growing day by day, bouncy locks beginning to form on her small, round head. Babbling happily. Arms reaching out to me. But I couldn't reach her. *I never can.*

My throat tightened. I stood up, mumbled something, and left the room, shutting the door tightly behind me.

Chapter 11

It took a while for me to recover from that prayer meeting. Thankfully, no one brought up my exit, so I did my best to forget the entire thing. Except, no one could forget that something had dramatically shifted for Babs. From that day forward, everything began to change for her. I watched in amazement at the metamorphosis as she emerged from her cocoon. She began devouring Bible study teachings, she willingly participated in the counseling sessions, and she engaged with the other clients. She even apologized to Nikki for her attitude and asked if they could be friends. No longer sullen, her personality emerged. She wasn't perfect of course, but the change was noted by everyone. Still inclined toward anger, she was learning to quickly acknowledge it and develop new ways of resolving conflict. Everyone agreed that "Bad Attitude Brilanna" no longer fit her, but when someone suggested we do away with the name "Babs," she jokingly threatened that she might really have a bad attitude if she lost her nickname. Babs was actually fun to be around.

I was baffled. Sharon was delighted.

"God showed up" was Sharon's explanation of what changed, and I couldn't deny that something big had happened that was inexplicable outside the work of God.

"That is what Mercy House is all about," she said one evening, as I sat with her and Rick on the porch. The pungent scent of spring onions in the freshly cut lawn lingered in the cool air.

I had come to cherish these "porch moments" with them. After everyone pitched in to clean up dinner, the girls busied themselves with their evening routines of bathing babies or studying, and that's when Rick, Sharon, and I would settle on the wide front porch. Rick and Sharon often sat on the loveseat, holding hands and sipping coffee or tea. I never felt like a third wheel though, because they genuinely seemed to want me there. Already, they were like surrogate parents to me, sharing words of wisdom, telling stories of their experiences, and often coaxing me, but never pushing, to let them into my world. Someday, I thought. But not yet. There was too much junk I didn't want them to see. I didn't want them to be disappointed.

"It was obvious that Brilanna was hurting," Sharon continued. "That tough exterior didn't fool anybody. It was simply a self-protection tactic. But Mercy House is a safe haven, a place where hurting people can let their guard down. And when that happens, healing begins. I never get tired of seeing that!" Her eyes were wide with excitement. "It's like a front row seat to watch God in live action!"

I smiled faintly, trying to catch her enthusiasm, but I didn't get it. The rhythmic motion of the porch swing sighed and creaked beneath me, as I focused on the soothing sherbet colors of the evening sky. I really wanted to understand.

"Real transformation," Rick said in agreement, patting Sharon's knee.

Why? Why was she transformed?

I couldn't shake the resentment I still had that God had given her two children and then that he cared enough to meet her personally, but not me. I couldn't reconcile what it was about me that didn't deserve his attention. I worked hard. I grew up in church. And, yes, I had been disenfranchised by the 'people of God' and stopped practicing my faith for a period of time, but then I left everything, or ran away from everything, to work in a ministry. Yet what had God done for me? The thoughts gnawed at me like the sharp teeth of a ravenous wolf on its prey.

I faked a yawn and stretched. "I think I'm going to head to bed early," I said, standing up. "I'll see you in the morning."

"Good night, Elle."

"Sleep well."

Alone in my room, I felt the rawness of my wounds. *God doesn't see you, Elle. You think what you do 'for him' matters even a tiny bit? How could it? You blew it a long time ago. Sure, you might have had a relationship with him when you were little, but you walked away.*

What about her? my rational mind argued back. I knew comparison was a thief, but it was the only justification I could latch onto. *How does someone with her background get to find favor with God?*

The voices in my head ate at me, continually, consuming me bit by bit until I feared only emptiness would remain.

* * * * * * * *

The next week after the Moms in Prayer meeting was over, Miss Susie sought me out. I had scheduled most of my desk work for the prayer hour so that I would have a legitimate reason to decline the expected invitation. Without any regard of whether or not what I was doing was important, she stepped into the office and placed her soft, pudgy hand on my shoulder. Annoyed, I pulled an earbud out of one ear and turned to look at her.

Compassion filled her moist eyes as she looked at me. "I see your pain, sweetheart, and I'm so sorry."

Her words surprised me and I looked away, hating the fact that her pity drew out the self-pity in me that I tried so hard to deaden. I said nothing, trying my best to swallow down the lump that arose in my throat, wishing she would leave. But her hand remained on my shoulder.

"I'm guessing you're mad at God, Elle, but don't push him away just because you don't understand what he's doing. He never promised us that life would be easy. In fact, he told us we would face trials. But he did promise us he will be with us always."

Angry tears stung my eyes and I clenched my teeth, trying to bite back a response.

"Take your disappointment to God," she continued.

"Don't disconnect from him. He's your source of life. He loves you, Elle."

I yanked out my other earbud and stood to face her, my eyes blazing. A toxic fury from deep down in my gut rumbled like hot lava until it erupted in scorching words. "What's the good of him even being God if he doesn't change circumstances for people—people he supposedly loves!"

It wasn't a question, yet the short, round, frizzy headed woman before me calmly took my clenched fist in her hands. Her compassion and serenity doused my anger to a cooling sizzle, and I fought hard to hold back tears.

"It's true that he can make things blissful for us," she said, "but that's what heaven is for—it's not why we're here. We have a mission in this world, Elle. You have a mission. This life is not about our comfort or our pleasure, and it's not a dress rehearsal for heaven—it's to bring more people into the Kingdom of God before this life is over. We are his kids living in enemy territory. Bad things are gonna happen. Can God stop it? Absolutely. But does he? Not always. Some things we will never understand this side of heaven. He tells us in his Word that as the heavens are higher than the earth, so are his thoughts above our thoughts. We can't understand the thoughts of God, but we can understand his heart. His heart is for you, Elle."

The words she fed me tasted bitter and I wanted to spit out some retort, but she continued. "I know you're disappointed in God. Cry out to him, honey. At least give him the chance to respond. It's not a fair fight when you get mad but walk away.

You may think you ended the fight, but all you did was prolong it. Your heart is still fighting him."

When I didn't respond, she turned and left the room as quietly as she had come in. Yet, her words echoed loudly in my mind.

You may think you ended the fight, but all you did was prolong it.

I closed the door behind her and leaned against it as the hot tears fell silently down my face. It was true. True with God and true with Ethan. I had walked away from Ethan, thinking that he was the problem. That leaving him behind would help me put my grief behind me. But it didn't. It was all still there, clamoring to steal my sanity, robbing me of life. I was angry. I was hurt. I needed answers. I decided I had no choice but to use the same tools I was giving to the clients. I would reach out to Kathy for a counseling referral.

Chapter 12

"I thought Boston summers were bad." I tugged at my T-shirt to create airflow as Rae and I climbed into the sauna-like van. We left the doors open until the air conditioning began to blow cold air.

Busyness had usurped my need for a counseling appointment, and the spring days had quickly given way to a stifling summer. The sticky heat of late June clung to the air and the afternoon sun bore down with a fierce intensity. Unfortunately, grocery shopping was relegated to mid afternoon to accommodate the lull in the daily schedule, and at that time of day, the heat felt like an oven.

"The thing about Texas weather is that it's not bad most of the year," Rae said. "Isn't a few months of heat much better than long, cold winters in Boston?" Rae adjusted the passenger air vents until her wispy bangs blew straight up from her forehead. "Besides, this heat is nothing that an iced latte can't cure!"

Rae had been my faithful companion in the weekly grocery run and always volunteered to get us coffee at the store cafe while I started on the list. It had become our thing, coffee and groceries. My favorite part was the drive there and back, despite the huge white van. Sometimes the conversation was light and fun. Sometimes we jammed out to the radio, which sounded surprisingly good for a fifteen-passenger vehicle. And sometimes the conversation went deep, with Rae sharing about her past life. What opioid addiction was like. How much she hated herself like that. How agonizing withdrawals were. And sometimes about her baby daddy, Jesse. I could tell she still had feelings for him. Even though she insisted that he was straightening up his life too, I made sure she remembered how hard it was for her to get better. And how good it was for little Melvin that his mom was healthy and he was not in a toxic environment. As much as I thought about it though, I still wasn't willing to talk to her about Ethan or the reason we had split.

Today when Rae returned from the cafe with my iced skinny double shot vanilla latte, a giddy grin covered half of her face. She hurried down the aisle toward me, a plastic cup in each hand, ice cubes jostling wildly in the beige liquid.

"Guess what!" she said excitedly, still half a row away from me. "I got a job!"

"What? How? Where?" I asked, baffled, unsure if that was okay. I knew Nikki worked at a salon and that a stable income was part of what was required to graduate from the Mercy House program. But I hadn't yet learned the procedure for clients acquiring jobs.

"At the cafe!" Rae said, excitedly. "The manager, her name is Rita, she just offered me a job and said I could start tomorrow!"

"Wow," I said, my voice mixed with surprise and concern. I took the latte from her before the contents escaped in her enthusiasm.

"You know it's part of what's required to graduate. Denise said I would need to start looking next month, but I can get started now!"

I sipped the cool liquid goodness. "Well, I guess our weekly coffee routine is paying dividends." I tried to sound happy, but I wondered what this would mean.

"Yeah, I'll be able to get you discounted coffee after I start!" Rae couldn't seem to keep her voice to a normal volume. "Wanna go meet Rita now so you can get things squared away?"

"Slow down and sip your coffee," I replied. "Denise will have to be the one to take care of the details or, at a minimum, tell me what I need to know."

"Can you at least get the ball rolling?" Rae begged, anxiously. "That would be so great to start tomorrow."

"What about Melvin?" I asked, wondering if she had even thought of what a sudden job would mean for her child.

"Maybe you could watch him for me until I get daycare sorted?" Rae looked at me imploringly over the rim of her cup, her eyes wide and childlike.

"Rae," I said, surprised by the firmness of my voice, "you can't just jump into this without working out the details first. You need to think about what this will mean for Melvin, and if this is even the best job for you. Besides," I added, softening my tone, "you know it won't bode well for me with Denise if I jump ahead of her procedures. She would love to find a reason to cut me loose."

Thankfully, that calmed Rae down and instead of continuing to pressure me, she scampered back to the cafe to pick up the paperwork while I finished shopping.

Selfishly, I tried to process what things would look like for me when Rae started working. And then what it would be like when she left Mercy House. I hadn't really considered it before, but over the past couple of months, I had come to rely on her presence, a built-in friend who kept life light-hearted, a companion who seemed to need me to provide her calmness as much as I needed her to lift my spirits. Moving on had to happen eventually, of course. Helping women stand on their own was what the program was all about.

That is why you're here, Elle, I reminded myself. But still, it wasn't something I looked forward to.

By the time I had made it through the checkout line, Rae was back at my side. I pushed the cart to the parking lot while she chatted excitedly about how she would get Denise onboard with the plan so she could start working. I only half-listened, caught up in my own thoughts as I methodically placed the bags in the back of the van.

When the cart was empty, Rae ran it back across the steaming pavement without even complaining about how far away I had parked. I climbed slowly into the driver's seat. The iced latte had worked its magic and, combined with the freezing temperature of Texas grocery stores, I felt chilled and even shaky. Closing the door without starting the engine, I shut my eyes and let the intense heat thaw my bones.

Rae broke in on my moment too soon when she opened the passenger door. "Geez, Louise!" she exclaimed. "What are you, a cat? Get this beast started!"

I laughed and complied, once again letting her humor pull me out of an impending funk.

* * * * * * *

Back at the house, after unloading the groceries, I spotted Kathy, the counselor. She had just finished an appointment with Babs and was on her way out the door. Without allowing myself the time to think, I pushed out of my comfort zone and stepped onto the porch.

"Kathy," I called after her. "Do you have a few minutes?"

She turned and smiled. "Of course."

I shifted my weight from one foot to the other, suddenly regretting my impulsive decision. I had curated a professional front with her and the other care providers who met with our clients. What would she think of me and my issues? But that was ridiculous. A professional wouldn't judge me. She would merely follow her training and provide the counsel needed. I pushed through my hesitancy. "I have some questions about counseling . . . for me . . . personally."

"That's great, Elle," she said easily, in a way that caused

me to expel the breath of air I hadn't realized I was holding. "I think counseling is a resource everyone should use. I'm glad you see that."

"I actually have some training in counseling," I offered, hoping to retain an appearance of togetherness. But then, reluctantly, I pushed myself to be vulnerable. "And I have been in the client chair as well. Would you like to sit?" I gestured toward the wicker porch chairs.

"Ooh, you've hooked me there," Kathy laughed. "I've always wanted to enjoy this beautiful porch."

She eased herself into a padded wicker chair, taking in the serene setting. Despite the heat, the porch was always refreshing. A breeze never failed to blow, wafting a mixture of gardenias and roses while the baskets of ferns danced happily. I sat in the matching chair across from her, giving her a moment to enjoy before I began my questions. But Kathy asked the first question.

"So, your background is counseling?" she asked, swinging her crossed-leg casually as if we were having a conversation about the weather, not about the pounding I felt in my chest. "Is it traditional counseling or freedom ministry?"

"Freedom ministry?" I tilted my head quizzically. I hadn't heard that term before.

"Yes, it's quite a bit different than traditional counseling," Kathy answered. "It isn't normally a part of a college syllabus. More commonly it's offered as a para-church ministry for people to receive inner healing. It's similar to what we do at CrossCounsel."

I was more than a little surprised. "Oh, I had assumed that Mercy House clients were receiving traditional counseling," I said, a tone of uncertainty in my voice.

"Well, we often work hand in hand with traditional counselors if clients require that," Kathy said. "I know it sounds strange," she added, apparently picking up on my concern, "but it actually makes a lot of sense. With your training in counseling, I'm sure you already know that emotions stem from our beliefs."

She waited for my nod and then continued. "We use a process that follows a client's negative emotion to the source of their pain, which is usually a lie they are believing."

I shifted uncomfortably in my chair, not sure what 'process' she meant. But she went on to explain. "It's as simple as encouraging the client to engage with their emotions and wait for a memory to surface. The memory serves as the container for the false belief which is driving the emotion."

I nodded again. That was common to most therapy. Maybe it wasn't so strange. "Can you give me an example of counsel or therapy you offer to help the client deal with their pain?" I was hoping to uncover some helpful nuggets, which might possibly suffice in lieu of an actual appointment. My counselor back in Boston had provided plenty of helpful tactics, like recognizing triggers and using breathing exercises, as well as wise counsel, such as encouraging me to incorporate the unlikely self-help technique of serving others—the very thing that started me on the path to Mercy House.

"Oh, we don't counsel," Kathy said.

But the name of your counseling service is CrossCounsel?

The unvoiced question must have been written on my face because she smiled as if she understood what I was thinking.

"We let the Holy Spirit do the counseling."

Wait— What???

"I'm sure that must seem unconventional to you," she continued, "but our counsel is actually not even needed with this method. That's the beauty of it. You see, with traditional counseling, you're helping a client reform habits and retrain their brain. But with our process, you are giving them tools that bypass that process and bring real freedom from negative emotions and bad habits."

I sat back in my chair and crossed my arms. Quickly rethinking my body language, I uncrossed them and forced them stiffly to the armrests, hoping it didn't convey the skepticism I felt. "Tools such as . . . ?"

"Really just an understanding of how their beliefs and emotions work together and how to uncover the lies that are driving their actions. Once we help them uncover the lie they are believing, we invite the Holy Spirit to speak truth there in that memory. It's just like the Bible says, the Holy Spirit is the counselor, and he will lead you into all truth. It's amazing to see the peace that people can experience when God speaks his truth right there in the midst of their emotional pain."

Did my face show that I had identified her as one of those

over-spiritual crazies? She seemed so normal. Like Sharon. But God speaking? That sounded very similar to what Miss Susie said. *"Let God respond."* If anyone could hear God, why had he never spoken to me? Why was I always having to guess what he wanted from me?

But, if this process she spoke about was an avenue to hear him, I desperately wanted to.

I felt like I was swinging on a pendulum. Wanting to learn more but wanting to run far away from the strangeness of it. I couldn't make sense of what was the right thing to do.

"That sounds too good to be true," I ventured.

"I know, right?" Kathy laughed, unfazed by or unaware of my skepticism. "Unfortunately, while it is simple, it's not easy. No one likes to face their pain. In fact, most people develop emotional blocks to protect them from feeling their pain. Those kinds of barriers can prove difficult, but we use the same process to help them break free of those as well as guardian lies."

I knew the terms and nodded but shifted uncomfortably in my chair. It might be fine for our clients, but I wasn't so sure it was for me. With my training, I doubted I could be a willing client without psychoanalyzing everything. But, then again, maybe that's what needed to happen. We wouldn't want to be subjecting our Mercy House residents to something that could negatively affect them.

"It all comes down to belief and choice," Kathy continued. "If the client is willing and chooses to go after the lies they are believing, they can be set free from the emotional pain that drives so much of their turmoil."

I recalled that Kathy had stopped meeting with Babs when she was unwilling. But after her change of heart, she had asked to meet with Kathy again, and honestly, she was on an amazing inner growth trajectory.

"People are like onions with layers upon layers of lies that have formed over time—even people without obvious trauma," Kathy said. "We all need continual counseling. I'm so glad you see that and want to pursue that for yourself."

"Actually, I'm not so sure," I said quickly. "I mean, yes, I agree about continued counseling, but I'm only familiar with normal—uh, traditional—counseling. So, thank you for clarifying, but I will need to think about it."

Kathy looked at me with an understanding smile. "I know it sounds strange. I thought the same thing when I was first exploring this process, but now that I have seen lasting transformation over and over, I can't deny the results. God truly works through this process." She sat back in her seat and shook her head. "But, I'm not trying to convince you, Elle—like I mentioned, it all comes down to *your* belief and choice. You have to choose for yourself or it won't work for you."

Her pitch was compelling, but I couldn't shake the fear of getting involved in a weird religious activity. I had already been burned by religion, and I was wary, to say the least. I needed to talk to Sharon. "Thanks," I said again. "But I think I should investigate a little further."

"That's a fantastic idea," Kathy said. "Hop on our website

and have a look around. We can even set up a meeting to discuss it further, if you want."

I stood, anxious to be done with the conversation. "Thanks for taking the time to explain things, Kathy. That's been helpful."

She stood as well, thanked me for the respite on the porch, and waved goodbye as she skipped lightly down the steps, still smiling good-naturedly.

Inwardly, I grimaced. That wasn't the type of counseling I was looking for.

* * * * * * *

Annoyance plagued me all through dinner. The convivial banter I usually enjoyed only served to postpone the time I could speak with Sharon alone. I was anxious to know if she was aware that CrossCounsel wasn't counseling.

But dinner dragged on. Nikki and Babs, who still suffered from a strained relationship, had teamed up to create a Latino-Cajun fusion meal, thanks to my strategic scheduling. It was gratifying to see them revel in shared compliments but frustrating that everyone helped themselves to more food to encourage the cooks.

I pushed my plate back in a move I hoped would end the convivium. But a sudden high-pitched squeal silenced everyone, and all heads turned toward Serena.

"Oh, oh, oh!" she exclaimed. "I think my water broke!"

"What? Really?" I asked, alarmed.

"What do you mean you 'think' your water broke?" Nikki asked.

"I don't know. My pants are wet."

Rae laughed. "You've cried wolf enough times, I 'think' you've just wet your pants," she said, using her fingers for air quotes. It was a mean comment but not unexpected from some of the quips Rae could let loose.

But tonight, Serena didn't take it well.

"You b—!" she shouted. She threw down her napkin and began to cry.

"Hey!" Sharon reprimanded the girls, as she hurried to Serena's side.

Babs stood up. "You need to apologize," she told Rae.

Nikki jumped to her feet. "What the—? What gives you the right to be holier than thou?" she said to Babs.

"That's enough!" Sharon said, her tone harsher than I ever heard it. Everyone went silent. "Serena, come with me," she instructed the weeping girl, falling into her trained midwifery role. "Let's take a look and get you changed." She turned to me briefly. "Elle, get things ready. You can go with me if it's time to take her to the hospital."

Rick, always the quiet strength, broke the tension when he stood and started clearing the plates. "Let's get this cleaned up, ladies," he said to the girls around the table. "We may have an exciting evening ahead."

Chapter 13

An hour later, the White Elephant was speeding toward the hospital with Serena's wails simulating a siren. I drove while Sharon sat with Serena on the second row, trying to calm the younger woman.

"We've planned for this, Serena." In the rearview mirror, I could see Sharon leaning toward the hysterical girl. "Your body was designed for this. It knows what to do. You just need to relax."

I breathed deeply, trying to relax myself as Serena's wails eased and then escalated over and over. I forced myself to focus on driving, although as frequently as we shuttled clients to the adjacent clinic, the White Elephant could probably drive the route itself. Like an expert ambulance driver, I pulled the white beast into the ER drop-off point and jumped out to assist Sharon and Serena. Then, hopping back in the vehicle, I drove off in search of the correct parking area. After much more time and difficulty maneuvering the beast through an adjacent parking garage, I strode quickly to the hospital entrance.

As I stepped through the automatic doors, cold, sterile air slapped me with an unsettling effect, and the scent of antiseptic assaulted my nostrils. I paused and looked from one hallway to the other, and back again. Should I follow the signs to the ER waiting room or go straight to the obstetrics wing?

I jumped at the ding of a nearby elevator. White glaring lights served to overload my senses.

Wiping my damp palms on my jeans, I inhaled but the breath caught in my throat. Why can't I . . . breathe?

I stood still, waiting for the constriction in my chest to ease. My tongue, cotton-like, weighed in my mouth and heat climbed from my neck to my face. My stomach roiled.

Was I going to pass out?

I shook off the feeling and made my way to an attendant at a nearby counter. "I'm looking for Serena Wilson. She was dropped off about ten or fifteen minutes ago at ER. She would have been heading to labor and delivery."

The woman behind the desk glanced up at me, her eyes oddly magnified behind her glasses. She asked for the spelling and punched at her keyboard as I gave it to her. I felt my cheeks as she concentrated on the screen before her. Clammy. Not good at all.

I shifted my weight from one foot to the other as the attendant continued to peck at the keyboard.

"I see she's checked in," she said finally. "Most likely she's still in the ER, but they should be taking her to Floor 4 momentarily. You can meet her there. The elevator bloc is down the hall to the right." She pointed me in the general direction. "Go to the fourth floor and follow signs for OBGYN."

"Thank you."

I repeated her instructions in my mind as I proceeded down the hall, my legs growing heavier with each step. Leaning against the elevator wall as it made its way to the fourth floor, I forced myself to breathe slowly and deeply.

The doors dinged open much too soon, and my knees buckled when I saw the all-caps: OBGYN.

I grabbed the wall and forced my body out of the elevator, my vision filling with black speckled dots. Reaching for a nearby bench, I folded my head between my knees in an attempt to stave off fainting. Then the memories came . . .

Cramping pain in my abdomen. Brown spots on my panties. Blood in the toilet. Long waits in a sterile waiting room. Wet, sticky gel on the ultrasound wand. Holding my breath as I watched the obscure gray screen, unable to make sense of it. Ethan gripping my hand.

Why was this so fresh? Almost a year had passed, a year of hell, a year of learning to cope. Maybe my friends were right. Maybe I was crazy for putting myself among moms and babies. How could I truly help them and be happy for them when I was stuck wishing for what they had?

Slowly, I lifted my head and reclined against the wall as the wave of nausea passed. I wanted to leave. I wanted so badly to find the nearest exit and run. Just run. But, in reality, that's what I'd already done. And the pain had caught up with me.

Oh, Jesus!

If it had been voiced, a passerby would have thought it

was an expletive. But my heart cried out instinctively. My go-to carryover from my younger years—crying out to Jesus when I felt like I was out of options. But I knew deep down there was only one option. Face the pain head-on. That was the real reason I was here. Everyone else thought I was coming to be a hero to this cause of saving the unborn, and I had even duped myself into thinking that many times over. Yet, I was the one I needed to save.

* * * * * * *

I don't know how long I sat like that, but finally the nausea passed and I was able to push the memories back into the deep recesses of my heart. When the emotion subsided, I stood and continued my search. I didn't even have to ask which room Serena was in. I followed the siren that rose and fell from a whimper to a wail. Unmistakably Serena. Standing outside the open door while the nurses worked, I watched silently as Sharon asked and answered questions and then spoke to Serena in a soothing voice. Sharon spotted me and stepped outside the door.

"She's only dilated to a two, so they won't be able to give her an epidural until she gets to a four or five," she told me in a hushed voice. "I think it's more fear than pain that she's feeling now, but they will give her some Demerol anyway, which should help her."

I nodded, certain that they were as anxious to quiet her

as everyone else was.

"If you want, you can hang out in the waiting room for a little while to see how quickly things progress. Maybe use the time to contact the Mercy House prayer partners to let them know her labor has started. And Denise. I'm here for the long haul, but I'll come out and give you updates periodically. Depending on how it goes, I may be here all night. If that looks likely, I'll let you know so you can head back to the house."

I nodded again.

Sharon put her hand on my shoulder. "You okay?" she asked, peering at me intently.

I averted my gaze. I wished I had opened up to Sharon. I wished she understood my turmoil around being here. Yet, I didn't want to tell her. And now certainly was not the time.

"Yeah," I answered. "Just a little overwhelmed."

Sharon smiled and squeezed my hand. "This is what it's all for! The vision of Mercy House—the training and love poured into the clients—all for this new little life about to enter the world! To make his world a better place."

I let myself catch the hope she shared. Returning the squeeze of her hand, I smiled. I could rise above the turmoil inside. What mattered right now was this new baby and helping his mom realize her strength. Yes, she was strong. She just didn't know it yet. And I was strong. I was. I had proven that. I just needed to remember it.

In the waiting room, I pulled my computer out of my bag and sent the messages that Serena was in labor. The minutes passed by slowly, and after scrolling through some news feeds, I typed in the web address for CrossCounsel. Carefully, curiously, I read. The information was compelling, I had to admit.

Emotions are connected to experiences in your life where you came to believe something negative. Now, when a similar situation arises, you feel the pain of that belief. That's good news, because even though the past can't be changed, your beliefs can.

Behavior changing is what I had always focused on. Learning to cope. Learning to manage the pain. But what I was reading made so much sense.

This transformational process goes beyond learning to behave differently. When your core beliefs change, you change without effort, from the inside out.

Riveted, I put in my headphones and watched testimonial videos of client after client who claimed to be free of the pain or fear or habit that had held them captive. Abuse . . . addiction . . . grief . . .

Could it be true? A glimmer of hope, ever so slight, sparked inside me. I did want to find out exactly what we were exposing our clients to anyway. I could wait to speak to Sharon, or I could just go ahead and book an appointment. I knew I had to find out more. I needed to. I needed something. I couldn't go on with this monster of grief hovering over me, waiting for just the right conditions to pounce on me again. I clicked the schedule button and quickly filled out the information without allowing myself time to rethink it.

Tonight had shown me how fresh the pain still was.

Being here. In this place. Waiting here. For this birth. It hurt. I didn't want it to, but it did. I wanted desperately to be happy for this young woman who had chosen to give birth to the fragile little life growing inside her. But this pain was consuming me . . . still.

I looked at the time on my computer. Over an hour had passed and still no word from Sharon. Should I be worried? No matter the pain I felt, I certainly never wanted anyone else to experience it. Sighing deeply, I opened the file with Sharon's next speech and set to work, aiming to take my mind off the present circumstances.

I was typing away, absorbed in the speech writing, when someone sat down beside me. Expecting Sharon, I looked over. "Oh . . ."

"Hi, darlin'. You doin' okay?"

Miss Susie. Somehow, she had picked up on my inner turmoil. Like one of those dogs that sniffs out cancer. Nosing, nudging as if I needed to be made aware of my pain.

"I'm fine." It sounded meaner than I meant.

"Good. Real good." Miss Susie nodded but didn't seem convinced.

"Serena is in labor." I attempted to deflect her probing.

"I got your text, honey."

Of course. Miss Susie was on the Mercy House prayer partners text thread. I had no idea who the numbers belonged to. They were simply ones I had been given to use for group messaging.

"I've already been by to see her and pray with her," she continued. "She'll be fine."

I nodded.

"It's you I'm concerned about."

I sighed, determined to be more polite. "Miss Susie, I appreciate that. Really, I do. But I'm fine."

I turned my focus back to my computer.

Miss Susie grew quiet. Too quiet. I wondered if I had hurt her feelings, but frankly, I didn't want to care. Unfortunately, that wasn't my nature. I glanced over at her, and she turned toward me. I focused on my computer screen again.

"Elle, I see you," Miss Susie said, emotion filling her voice. Her statement caught me off guard, but I didn't flinch. "And more importantly, God sees you."

The words stabbed at my heart.

"He sees the hurt you've experienced," she continued. "And he also sees that you've put yourself in a place to minister to those very people who have what you've lost."

I sucked in a breath, holding my jaw taut.

"That's selflessness, Elle. That kind of selfless sacrifice, God knows well. It takes great strength and great love. You are strong, Elle. You are brave."

Dang it, Miss Susie! The tears crept into my eyes and I swiped hastily at them as they began to spill over.

The older lady circled her pudgy arm around me and pulled me close, like a mother hen tucking her chick under her wing. I was stiff and unbending, but her arm remained steady around my shoulders.

"He wants to give you peace, Elle. Philippians 4:6 and 7 instructs us to tell God what we need, thank him, and receive his peace. You can receive his peace even before you get an answer. Just give it all over to him, sweetheart."

"Tell him what I need?" I could feel the anger rising. "Tell him what I need?? I needed my baby." A lone sob escaped my lips.

Miss Susie's only response was to pull me closer. Weary, so weary, I sunk into her embrace and began to weep.

"Let it out, honey," she crooned, her breath warm against the top of my head. "Let it out."

Unlike the memories I pushed back into tucked away places of my heart, I closed my eyes and let the tears seep out, running freely down my cheeks, dripping softly from my chin. The emotions rolled up to an overflowing level as I yielded to them. My shoulders shook with the heavy, cleansing sobs that escaped, but Miss Susie held me steady.

"It's okay. Let it all go," she whispered gently.

It had been a long time since I'd felt loved like this. Since I had let myself be loved. And in between the deep-gutted pain came a sweetness that I couldn't quite define.

Miss Susie stayed with me in the waiting room until Sharon entered the waiting area, beaming with the news that Baby Silas had been born. A healthy 7 pounds, 9 ounces, he and his mom were both doing great. By the time Sharon and I left the hospital, a new day had begun. We rode in silence through the twilight streets, Sharon in exhausted elation, and I in sub-dued reflection. I really had gained some measure of peace as I sobbed out my pain in Miss Susie's arms. Yet, I knew deep down, I hadn't let it all go. How could I? If I didn't have the sadness, I would have absolutely nothing left of my baby.

The night had been a painful reminder that life goes on, and my biggest fear was that I would move on, too, forgetting that precious life I had once carried in my womb.

Chapter 14

The night of Serena's delivery was a turning point for me in more ways than one. I no longer felt like the "newbie" among the staff or the clients. I had become one of them. I was family. And with each passing day, Mercy House felt more and more like home to me. A safe place. A sanctuary. I had known it would be. But there was way more to it than the beautiful old home or even the sense of purpose it held for the women and children it sheltered and those of us who worked there. It was nearly a tangible sense of peace. Almost inexplicable, really.

Comfort.

Hope.

Peace.

I hadn't forgotten my wistful prayers about getting me to this place, and although I strategically avoided the Moms in Prayer group each week, I did thank God in the quiet moments. There was something to that thing Miss Susie had said about thanksgiving being a key to joy. I felt better than I had in a very long time. Even attending church with the girls wasn't terrible. I still cringed admitting this to myself, but I actually enjoyed it some—even the music.

Because of Miss Susie, I pulled out the leather-bound Bible my mother had given me on the day I was baptized. It had my name engraved on it and inside were the handwritten words: "With love from Mom — Numbers 6:24-26." It resided as a new staple on my bedside table, and I often opened it at night to look up the scriptures Miss Susie texted me.

In fact, I was doing so well that I had postponed the counseling session with Kathy. Twice. I tried to cancel, but she strongly cautioned me that, even if I was feeling better, if I hadn't dealt with the core issues, they likely lurked beneath the surface, waiting for a trigger to set them off again. "Don't give up on the pursuit of freedom, Elle," Kathy told me the last time I tried to cancel. "Nothing compares to the lasting peace that can be yours." So, I simply delayed my appointment.

Maybe it was the deeper connections with others that helped, but I knew I was in a healthier place. Rae and I often had late-night chats after the house settled into the deep quiet that sleep brings. Sometimes we crept onto the Juliet balcony through the tall, door-like windows that struggled to open. There in the narrow space between the stained glass and the old wooden turned posts, we reclined beneath the inky sky searching for constellations and chewing on Trollies. We talked comfortably like old friends. Many times, I came close to telling her about Ethan and the baby, but something deep inside kept that guarded. Protected. A sorrowful, secluded part of me that once was, but couldn't be resurrected. I still hadn't said anything to Sharon, either. It seemed pointless to dredge that up now, especially when it seemed I had finally turned a corner.

Late one night, after lights were out and I was settled into bed, reading by lamplight, I heard a tap on my door. A code tapped out in one whole beat, four staccato, and two long beats. Rae.

I threw back the covers and padded to the door. We were overdue for a late-night chat, and I wanted to hear how she was feeling. Denise had approved her job at the coffee shop as soon as Melvin was settled into daycare. Her first day on the job was tomorrow.

The old door gave a low groan as I pulled it open.

"Got time to talk?" Rae whispered.

"Sure," I smiled.

I opened the door wide for her to enter, but then as I tried to close it, I felt resistance pushing back.

Peering through the crack was Serena's face.

"Me too?" she whispered.

I laughed and opened the door for her to come in.

"I need a break from that child of mine," she confessed, flopping herself onto my high, plush mattress as Rae seated herself comfortably at the foot.

Silas's newborn cries were familiar to everyone in the house now, so we understood the struggles she was having.

"I need some grownup time . . . even if the grownups include those who act like a baby," she added surly.

We all knew she was talking about Rae's comment the night Silas was born. The cold shoulder she'd been giving Rae since then was not one she intended to go unnoticed. But Rae had been so busy, she hadn't taken time to clear the air.

"Deserved," Rae acknowledged, shaking her head regretfully. "I'm sorry for setting you off when your water broke. Sometimes what I think will lighten things up hits hard instead."

"Mmm-hmmm," Serena said.

"Hey, I'm being vulnerable here," Rae said. "I apologized and this is where you say 'I forgive you.'"

Serena rolled her eyes. "It feels like you don't even think about the person at the butt of your jokes. Instead, all you care about is making the crowd laugh."

"That's not true," Rae said defensively. But then she conceded. "Okay, maybe it is, but I never mean for people to get hurt."

"Well, they do," Serena said pointedly, adding a sassy wag of her head.

"Look, I'm really sorry," Rae said. "Not trying to make an excuse for it, but the truth is I've had a lot going on in my head, and I guess jokes—even mean ones— are my way of coping. I'm sorry you were on the receiving end."

"Okay, I forgive you," Serena said with exaggerated emphasis. "I'm done with baby problems. Let's move on. What you got going on? Is that why you're sneaking in Miss Elle's room?"

For a moment I thought they had forgotten they had taken over my room or even knew I was there. I settled myself back in my spot on the bed, propped up against the feather pillow.

"Yeah," I prompted. "What's up, Rae?"

Rae shook her head, rolling her eyes dramatically. "A lot actually. Too much. There's a lot of stuff that I haven't told you, and . . . I probably should."

"I'm listening."

"Well, my job at the cafe—"

A peck at the door interrupted her. And the door opened slightly. "Can we come in too?" It was Judith and Babs.

I waved them in. "The more the merrier, right?"

Giggling like schoolgirls, they shuffled in. "Trying to have a party without us?" Babs chided good-naturedly. She pulled my desk chair close to the bed, and sat down with her fuzzy slippered feet propped up on the wooden bedrail. Judith heaved her baby weight onto the foot of my bed next to Rae. Her pregnant belly seemed to have doubled in size over the last few weeks.

"That baby must really be growing," I said, gesturing to her tummy. "Won't be long now!"

Judith's face gave me pause—not excited like most expectant moms. *Of course she wouldn't be excited.* I kicked myself mentally. She was giving her baby up for adoption. I hurried to change the topic by bringing up Serena's birth story.

"I'm sure it won't be nearly as dramatic as Si-rena," I said. The girls all laughed at the nickname.

"Hey!" Serena laughed. "The pain was real!"

I went on to describe the harrowing drive as I coped with the wails coming from the backseat.

"Yeah, yeah," Serena said. "Just be glad you were in the

driver's seat and not trying to push a basketball outta your vagina."

I winced, realizing that wasn't a great thing for Judith to hear either.

"Maybe we should get back to Rae's story," I suggested.

"Bedtime story?" Judith asked, reminding me how young she was.

"More like a confession session," Serena answered.

"Ooooh, juicy!" Judith gleefully rubbed her hands together. "I have missed watching Judge Judy. Denise turns off the TV every time she sees me watching it. The most drama I get now is an episode of *The Voice*."

"Rae was just about to spill, but now that she has an audience, look out," Serena quipped. "She probably has some jokes to tell instead."

"Can you let that go already?" Rae said. Her voice was strained and oddly void of her normal sarcasm.

Serena raised her hands in mock surrender, and Rae sighed deeply. "I'm sorry. Alright?" She clutched her head, combing her fingers through her silky black hair as if she were hot and needed fresh air.

This was not at all like Rae. Something really must be wrong, I thought, regretting the decision to let the others in. "Maybe we should cancel this party," I suggested.

"No, no," Rae said. "I'm just stressed. It's a lot, you know. A big change. I haven't held a real job since I was waitressing almost four years ago. And then there's Jesse." Her voice softened. "I . . . well, I've been thinking about him a lot lately."

"Do tell," Judith encouraged.

"He's doing so much better. Holding a steady job. He's really cleaned himself up." Her voice was hopeful, even animated as she talked about him, trying to convince us how good he was.

My jaw clenched as I tried to remain expressionless, but I wanted to remind her of all that she seemed to be forgetting about him.

"Have you been in contact with him?" I asked pointedly.

Rae dropped her head. "I've heard from him."

"Where? How?" I asked. Instantly, I was on alert. I knew the danger clients faced when they put themselves back in their old environment too soon. And obviously, Rae had broken protocol. She had no access to a cell phone or the internet, but somehow she had managed to connect with him.

Rae raised her head and looked at me, her eyes narrowing. "Am I being interrogated now?"

"No," I said quickly. But my questions did sound like Denise, eager to find out where she had stepped out of bounds and nail her for it. Yet I only wanted to protect her. Dialing it back, I said, "Just tell us about it. I'm listening."

"You know, never mind," Rae said, obviously frustrated. So unlike her easy-going nature.

I berated myself as Rae clammed up. The other girls looked at one other uncomfortably, even as Judith lamented the end of confession-session.

Then Babs spoke. "Well, I'll take the confession stand."

Everyone looked at her expectantly, except Rae who fidgeted with the hem of her T-shirt. Babs had continued to come out of her shell, speaking freely about her past life and all that she was learning now that she was studying the Bible.

"I don't want y'all to think bad things about me, but Miss Susie says confession cleanses the soul, and I want to be clean."

"Well, go on, then," Serena prompted her.

Babs wrinkled her mouth in a worried frown that punctuated a dimple in her ample cheek. "I ain't admitted this to anyone before," she said. "I thought I was fixed, ya know? Miss Susie and Miss Debra talking about how the Bible says our old sinful self is dead and buried . . . Well, my old self keeps resurrecting. I just don't get it. Especially anger. I think I'm over and done with it, and then something lights me up and I feel myself gettin' so angry I don't know if I can control it."

"How's that a confession?" Serena said. "Everybody gets angry."

"Well, it scares me sometimes. I know what rage can do." She shivered with the thought. "It scares me. Especially with a little one on the way. I remember those baby cries when you're so tired you can't even see straight. And this demanding lil' tyrant won't be quiet so you can sleep or even think. Has to be fed. Has to be changed. Doesn't care how you feel. And you get so angry—" Her voice caught in her throat. She shook her head as tears made their way around her full cheek and splashed down her neck. "I deserved for my baby to be taken away from me." She let out a sob. "And I'm so scared." She clenched her eyes shut as if to hold back the fear that made its way out of her lips. "So scared I won't deserve to take care of this one neither."

Silence permeated the room. Eyes were downcast. Answerless. Some understood. Some of us didn't.

Finally, Judith spoke. "Maybe just talking about it helps. Everyone struggles with something. Maybe some more than others. But talking helps. Like you said, confession is good for the soul." She paused, rubbing her swollen abdomen before she added softly, "After all, we are only as sick as our secrets."

Rae caught my eye and held the gaze momentarily.

We are only as sick as our secrets. Such profound words from the youngest among us. We all seemed to feel the weight of them.

"That's deep," Serena said, thoughtfully.

Each sat quietly, contemplating, until Judith broke the silence with a giggle.

"Okay, well, I'll confess then." We all looked at her, and I wondered what more wisdom this young sage would share. "Those aren't my words." She grinned sheepishly. "That's just something I heard from Judge Judy."

An eruption of laughter and a few thrown pillows broke the contemplative moment.

Chapter 15

I bided my time, waiting for and dreading the counseling appointment with Kathy. The girls made it sound both horrifying and exhilarating, and they admitted to both loving and hating it. It wasn't like normal counseling, they said. You followed your own memories to painful places and kept digging deeper until a lie-based belief was exposed and truth was invited in.

"God will speak to you," Kiya told me when I confided I had booked an appointment. "You might not think you can hear God, but he will speak to you in a way that you can."

I had grown to admire her quiet strength. And in spite of Denise's repeated warnings to not fraternize with the clients, I had been spending more time with her since Rae had taken the job at the grocery store cafe. Between Rae's classes and job, the only time she and I were together was when I was driving her to the daycare or her job.

Little Melvin spent long hours at daycare while his mom worked. It hadn't become easier to be around him, but I couldn't stop myself from wanting that. He was growing so fast and each milestone affected me with a heart pang, wishing I could have seen my own child grow in the same way. I often found excuses to hoist him onto my hip. He had even begun reaching for me whenever I was close by.

One afternoon, Kiya joined me on the floor beside Melvin, as he enjoyed some tummy time. I was watching him while Rae got ready for work. Since Rae had started her job, she took a lot more time on her looks. No more sweatpants and headbands for her, which translated into plenty of time for me to be with Melvin.

Ki thoughtfully rubbed her huge belly as Melvin cooed and gurgled. She was only twenty-two weeks along, but she looked like she'd swallowed a basketball.

"Is one of the twins trying to answer him?" I joked.

She laughed. "Nah, they are actually pretty quiet for a change." She shifted her weight to the opposite hip, propping herself up with one thin brown arm while the other rested protectively on her abdomen. "Elle, I've been wanting to ask you something."

"Of course," I said easily. "Ask me anything."

She cleared her throat and looked at me. "I was wondering if you would be there with me when the twins are born. Will you be my person?"

My stomach lurched with an excruciating effect that made me feel almost nauseous.

Be with her? In the delivery room?

I quickly turned my attention to Melvin to hide my reaction in case it showed on my face. Reaching over to move a toy within his reach, I bought a moment to compose myself.

"Wow," I said finally, fumbling for words. "I wasn't

expecting that. I thought Thomas was going to be there."

Her silence caused me look at her. She shook her head, her eyes downcast. "No," she said quietly. "He won't be there."

"I'm sorry," I said. I knew she had wanted the twins' father there. "What about your mom? Is she coming?" Surely there was someone better equipped than me.

"It's okay," she said.

I felt awful.

"No, really, it's not a put-off. I just don't want to take someone else's rightful place," I lied.

"I want you there," Kiya said. "You're like the older sister I never had. The smart, sane one that could have helped me go in another direction if you'd been around all my life."

I forced a smile. "That means a lot." I reached over and put my hand on hers.

"So . . . ?" she said, looking at me with a quizzical smile. "Is that a yes?"

Tears sprang to my eyes suddenly as I imagined myself in the birthing room with her. *Could I do it? Could I be strong when she needed me the most?*

"Elle? What is it?"

I shook my head. "Nothing, nothing," I said, quickly recovering my composure. "I'm just honored that you asked me to be your person. Let's set a time to discuss your whole birth plan in depth, okay? There's a lot to consider since they'll probably schedule a C-section for the safety of the twins. So, talk about it later? Right now, I gotta get this little pumpkin and his mama out the door. We don't want to be late!"

I stood to my feet and scooped Melvin up into my arms. Kiya remained seated on the floor and I could feel her eyes watching me as I hurried away, the old wooden floorboards creaking beneath my steps.

* * * * *

I waited outside the employee entrance at the cafe much longer than usual after Rae's shift was due to end. The parking area was dimly lit, and I had long since turned off the radio so that the white elephant's battery wouldn't give out. It wasn't out of the ordinary for Rae to work past her shift, but she normally let me know if she would need to be picked up later. Agitated, I looked at my watch. I knew Melvin's daycare would be closing soon.

Finally, I flung open the door to the van and marched up to the employee entrance. The cafe had closed nearly an hour ago, so I banged on the door until someone answered. The shift manager, Rita, opened the door, her haggard eyes meeting mine with a question.

"Hey, Rita," I said before she could speak. "I don't want to leave you in a bind cleaning up, but Rae's way past her shift and we need to get her son from daycare."

The woman's expression changed to surprise.

"Honey, Rae called in sick today. That's why I'm here so late. We've been shorthanded all evening."

I felt the blood draining from my face.

Confusion.

Questions.

Shock.

Betrayal.

Anger.

I cycled through the emotions until the last one settled on my lips in a grim line.

Rita saw it too and her face changed from surprise to regret. "Oh, honey, I'm sorry. I remember now the sick call should have come from you. But Rae, she's . . . she never gave me reason to doubt her."

"Rita, you know all schedule changes go through me."

"I'm so sorry. I should have known there was something up when she took it so hard that I fired Jesse."

"Jesse?! Jesse, her baby daddy?"

Rita looked taken aback. "Jesse, my barista, who came in high last week."

My stomach was in knots. Everything was making sense now. The offers to get me coffee from the store cafe every time we went grocery shopping. Her excitement to start this job. The way she'd been taking such extra care with her looks.

"When did she call in?" I asked, seething.

"This mornin'. Before the lunch rush."

"I dropped her off this afternoon." I could kick myself that I didn't see this coming. She had asked me to drop her at the front entrance to the store. I clenched my fists. *Winsome Rae.* All her ways to get people to do what she wanted without ever realizing she was taking advantage of them. I couldn't blame Rita. I'd been duped big time.

"Thanks, Rita," I said. "I'm going to go get the baby. I will keep you posted about her future work schedule."

I walked briskly back to the van and slammed the door shut. I buckled my seat belt, started the engine, and jerked the stick shift to reverse. Just as I turned my head to back out, I saw Rae. She stumbled up to the van and knocked on the passenger window, grinning. Fuming, I hit the unlock button and put the van back into park as she opened the door.

"What are you thinking???" I unloaded.

Rae giggled.

"Rae!" I shouted. "Look at me! What are you doing? Lying? Conniving? Sneaking around? Getting high? Jesse? Don't you realize what you're risking?"

She looked at me, no longer smiling, her eyes wide. Like a child. In so many ways, she was like a child. Her lip quivered and her eyes filled with tears. "Don't be mad."

"You are risking everything!"

"I love him, Elle. I love him so much."

"Rae," I took a deep breath. "I know you love him. But you have to think of what is best for Melvin. You could lose Melvin over this. If CPS knew, they would come and take him away."

"You won't tell, will you?"

I sighed and put the van back into gear. "We will talk about this again tomorrow. Right now, we have to go get your son."

The next morning after breakfast, I requested a meeting with Rae in my room. She plopped down comfortably on my bed. I was too tense to sit. Instead, I paced back and forth in front of her. Fists clenched.

"Look, I messed up," she said. "I'm sorry. It won't happen again."

"Rae, how can I believe that?" I stopped mid-pace and turned to face her. "You lied to me. I thought I was your confidant. And then to find out you've been seeing Jesse secretly and getting high?"

"I knew you'd never understand about Jesse, okay? I couldn't talk to you about him. But the drugs—that only happened last night, I promise. I know how bad that crap is. It nearly ruined my life. I will not let myself go back down that path."

"Rae, you're playing with fire. You've told me yourself that Jesse is trouble. He's an addict and he will draw you back down that same road."

"It's not like that. He's working hard to get better."

"Apparently not hard enough to keep his job."

"Look, Elle, Jesse loves me," Rae said, her voice firm, infuriating me further. "And he loves Melvin. He wants to make this work, and I do too. We want to be a family."

"If he loved you, Rae—if he loved either of you, he would not put Melvin at risk of being taken away from you." I knew the words were too harsh as soon as they left my mouth. But she needed to hear it. "Rae," I said more softly, "When you're sneaking around hiding stuff from your friend, you know what you're doing is wrong."

Rae got up from the bed. "Hiding stuff? Tell me, Elle, what kind of friend is it who hides stuff?" She squared off to face me, hands flung out at her sides. "You say you're my friend, but you're the one who is the master at hiding your past. It's obvious that you wear this plastic mask, unwilling to share your stuff. How do you expect me to trust you when you can't be real with me?"

With that, she turned and left the room, closing the door hard behind her. I stood staring at the door for several minutes. The weight of her words fell like heavy blocks breaking the surface of my soul. Slowly, deeply they sunk until they found a place to settle in the niches of my heart. Could others trust me with their pain when I wasn't willing to trust them with mine?

Chapter 16

I was sick for days, agonizing over what to do about Rae. I couldn't put Melvin in danger of being taken away. As long as he was at Mercy House, he was safe, but if Denise or Sharon had any idea what had happened, Rae would be kicked out of the program and CPS would be involved. Yet if I didn't say anything and Rae continued down this road, both her and Melvin's lives could be ruined.

Alone in my bed, I tossed and turned. Sleep finally came, but I was startled awake by another bad dream for the third night in a row. They all had the same theme: I was on track with something, but then made a decision that ended up being the wrong one. Each time I woke with gut-wrenching regret filling my stomach in the form of acid.

How could I make the right decision? So much was at stake.

I pulled myself from the bed and resorted to breathing techniques in effort to calm my churning stomach. One positive thing was that I had finally confirmed my appointment with Kathy. I wished I could ask her advice, but I knew too much was in jeopardy. Still, I hoped sorting through my own thoughts would bring clarity.

In spite of my preoccupied mind, the work never stopped in assisting clients. Later that afternoon, I picked up Judith from an ultrasound appointment. It was the last planned one before her due date, and she'd been joined by the adoptive parents to view the baby's growth.

"How did it go?" I asked.

She was solemn. Her eyes grew moist. Finally, she smiled, "It's getting real."

"Yeah?" I was amazed at the maturity of this young woman. When most girls her age were getting a driver's license and going to high school football games, she was battling swollen ankles and back pain.

She nodded and swiped away a tear.

I put the White Elephant in drive and pulled away from the curb, allowing her privacy with her emotions. But I remembered what she had told Babs about how it helps to talk.

"A penny for your thoughts," I said gently, keeping my eyes on the road.

Judith offered a short laugh. "That's what my aunt used to say when I was little." She grew quiet again, but then sighed. "There's a swirl of thoughts . . . and emotions."

"Well, tell me about it," I prompted. "Just note that I didn't say 'penny per thought'—I'm not a rich woman, you know." I smiled and glanced over at her.

Judith looked out the window at the passing scenery. "Honestly, I try not to think about it . . . and I do a pretty good job of that until these appointments come along. But I got to see him today. And he's really growing. Looks like a real baby." She laughed at her own comment.

I remained quiet. Waiting.

"Sometimes I wonder if I'm doing the right thing."

I swallowed, trying not to let my own emotions surface. How well I knew those thoughts. Those feelings. Always trying to make the right decision, trying to make everyone happy, questioning my decisions, and always fighting regrets. Always. I struggled with it now in Rae's situation, and I had struggled with it through the first trimester of my own pregnancy. But my thoughts had been opposite of Judith's. Was I doing the right thing to keep this baby? Who was I, a naive college student, to think I could be a decent mother? What would people think— especially my dad and the church people—about the scandal of being pregnant and unmarried? What future would Ethan be giving up if we got married like he suggested? None of the questions gave deep consideration to the little human growing inside me, and the guilt of that after the subsequent miscarriage left me with deep shame.

But here beside me was an even younger woman fighting guilt and shame for giving her baby up.

"What made you decide to go through with the pregnancy in the first place?" I asked, shaking away my own thoughts. I assumed abortion had been a consideration for a sixteen-year-old girl in her situation.

"There was never any question about it," Judith replied

with a shrug. "Letting myself get pregnant was a dumb mistake. It just . . . happened." I nodded. Knew that one well. "I got myself in that situation, and it wasn't the baby's fault."

I blinked, surprised. How could a child arrive at a more grown-up conclusion than myself or my friends had? I wanted to cry. I wanted to gush out to her that she was right, she was brave. And that one mature decision had saved herself a lifetime of heart-crushing guilt. But I didn't know what she would face after the adoption. I couldn't imagine what it would be like to carry a part of yourself for forty weeks, to feel him or her move, and to know that you would be giving up the opportunity to comfort and hold them as they grew. Far from how I initially judged her, I realized now what a selfless gift it was that she was giving. The gift of life to the baby and the gift of love to the adoptive parents. She was incredibly brave.

"It was the right decision," I said hoarsely, after I found my voice. I looked over at her and nodded affirmatively. "And I think you're making the right decision now, too."

Her eyes filled with tears before she turned her head back to the passenger window, where the glass reflected her face. She looked so young. I wanted to help her. Comfort her somehow. Shield her from pain. But I knew she was strong on her own.

"I don't know what the future holds," I said, "but I think you're giving this baby the best chance for a good life. That's the gift every mom wants to give her baby."

"But—" her voice broke. "I won't be a mom. I'll be giving that title away too."

"You will always be a mom," I said, my voice surprisingly adamant. And no doubt she would feel the pain of loss much like I did.

My heart hurt for her, as I thought about it. It hurt for women in crises and the complications of women who had storied pasts.

Things sure could get blurry. I could understand why people felt compelled to have abortions even. But no matter the way a child is lost, it is most definitely a loss to the empty arms that will one day ache.

Maybe a celebration of life would be just the thing to help Judith. I made a mental note to contact our partner ministry, Embrace Grace. The people who volunteered in that organization would know just the right way to celebrate this brave, young mom.

"Here," I said, reaching into the center console of the White Elephant. "I have just the thing for you." One hand on the wheel and eyes on the road, I fished out a plastic pouch of Trollies. "These have been known to cure all sorts of ailments. I never believed it until I tried one myself. One bite of this deliciously sugary sour miracle and all problems dissolve."

* * * * * * *

I contemplated my conversation with Judith until Rae knocked on my bedroom door that evening. Begrudgingly, I opened it. I knew she was going to press me again for an answer about returning to the cafe. At my request, Rita had given her a few days off, and thankfully Denise never questioned her schedule. I wasn't ready to answer yet, but after thinking long and hard about Judith's dilemma, I knew I needed to follow her example and make a decision and stick with it, no matter what consequences may ensue.

Rae came in and I closed the door as she plopped on my bed.

Her eyes held the question as she looked at me. Neither of us spoke.

Turning away from her, I massaged my temples, trying to think. As angry as I was at her, I couldn't bear the idea of her leaving, nor could I stand the thought of little Melvin gone. Where would he be sent? I couldn't shake the thought of him sobbing hysterically in an unfamiliar place, without his mom, and without the comfort of everyone and everything he knew, including me.

"I hate that you've put me in this position!"

"How many times do I have to tell you I'm sorry before you believe it? I'm really, really sorry, Elle. It was a stupid mistake, and I won't let it happen again. Please, Elle, I'm begging you. Please don't tell. Let's just forget it ever happened."

"I could lose my job over this!"

"But you won't if you just let me go back to work. No one will ever need to know."

"How can I trust you, Rae? How can I believe that you won't be sneaking off with Jesse again?"

"Elle, listen to me." Rae stood and faced me, placing her hands on my shoulders. "I swear to you, I won't see him again."

Finally, I gave in.

Against my better judgment, I smoothed everything over with Rita at the cafe. She agreed to notify me if Jesse ever showed up there, and Rae was allowed to return to work, keeping her place in the program. Sharon and Denise were none the wiser. And I was plagued by guilt.

Chapter 17

I fidgeted nervously, my demeanor completely opposite of Kathy's. She sat in a chair across from me, her legs crossed comfortably, notepad resting on her lap. I'd set the meeting in her office rather than at the house where she met with the Mercy House clients.

Kathy reached over and placed a box of Kleenex beside me.

"It's natural to cry as you allow yourself to feel through your memories," she said. "Don't try to hold back. Let the emotion come. What you are feeling here in the present links back to a little girl who was hurt and wounded. That little girl started believing something that causes the reactions you feel even to this day. Try to let the memories surface so that you can uncover those false beliefs and replace them with truth. Your emotions are the bridge to the memories, so just let yourself feel, Elle."

I nodded stiffly and reached for a Kleenex, which I began twisting in my hands, thankful for something to keep them from shaking.

"There's no need to be nervous," Kathy said gently. "You're the one in control here. We will let your emotions lead the way. I'm going to pray and then you can begin talking out what you're feeling, okay?"

I nodded again and closed my eyes as Kathy began to pray. "Father, thank you for meeting with us here. Thank you for your incredible love for Elle and for the sacrifice of your Son Jesus that set her free. Your Word tells us that it is for freedom that she has been set free, so Father, I thank you for the courage you've given her to pursue that freedom and fullness that you are waiting for her to step into. Lord, would you just encourage her heart now as she works through painful memories?"

Kathy stopped. She hadn't said the obligatory 'amen,' so I kept my head bowed, waiting.

"Just keep your eyes closed, Elle, if that helps you focus inward," she told me gently. "Let yourself feel whatever emotion is right there on the surface."

Immediately, salty tears burned the inside of my eyelids. The emotion was never too far away and the invitation caused it to rise, unhindered. I dabbed the Kleenex at the corners of my eyes.

"What is that emotion you're feeling, Elle?"

I shook my head. I wasn't sure. Sadness. Guilt. Loss. Grief. Anger. Confusion. So much.

"It's okay," Kathy replied to my silence. "Just let yourself connect there. What memories are surfacing with those feelings?"

Flashes of anger and betrayal brought the scene with Rae to mind and there was sadness all at the same time. I couldn't tell her about Rae though. I couldn't tell anyone.

"There's just a lot," I said hoarsely. "So many different thoughts."

"That's normal," Kathy said, obviously trying to put me at ease. "Try to connect with the earliest memory. When was the first time you can remember feeling that way? You might not think it connects but just go with whatever comes up."

As soon as the words left her mouth, an image of my childhood friend came into my mind. Marley. I hadn't thought of her in years.

"When I was probably seven or eight," I answered. Marley was my age and lived next door to us. I liked her okay, but Mom liked her more—at least that's what I secretly thought.

"Put yourself in that little Elle's shoes," Kathy said. "What's she feeling or thinking?"

Mom always invited Marley to come over to the house to play with me, even when I would have rather played by myself. It wasn't until later that I realized Mom was probably trying to avoid time with me. Since I had no siblings, I always wanted her attention, and when she took the time to play with me, I was so happy. But more times than not, she called Marley's mom to see if Marley could come play with me.

"Marley would be good at that. Marley would enjoy doing that with you. Marley this. Marley that."

It got to the point that even her name caused me to bristle. I could feel the same old spite. One time, I asked Mom to play Barbies with me. It was always the best when she played. But she huffed and told me I needed to learn how to make friends. Then she went to the phone and called Marley's house. But Marley had gone to another friend's house. Mom's face pinched into a scowl as soon as she hung up the phone. *"Why can't you be more like Marley?"*

"What's going on in there, Elle?" Kathy asked. I wasn't sure how long I had been thinking.

"I'm angry."

"Who are you angry with?"

"Marley."

"What would happen if you could let go of that anger toward Marley?"

I looked up, confused by the question.

"What is the anger doing for you?" Kathy said. "Anger is a protective emotion. If you were to let go of it, what else would you be feeling there?"

I gave Kathy a blank look.

"Let's try this," she said. "Close your eyes again and reconnect with that little girl. Let yourself feel that anger toward Marley. What is that little girl believing right there?"

I closed my eyes. I did feel it. And I knew what it meant. "Mom loves Marley more than me."

"Are you willing to hear God's perspective on that?"

I hesitated, then answered, my voice inflecting almost to a question. "Yes . . ."

"Lord, what do you want Elle to know? She believes her mom loves Marley more than her. Is that true?"

No. I knew it wasn't true. I saw Mom in my mind's eye.

Her bedroom door closed. I could hear the clinking of glass that I knew was the bottle of alcohol she kept in her closet. And then it was like I was seeing through her door, a broken woman. Compassion filled my heart. It wasn't that she loved Marley more. It wasn't that she didn't want to be my friend. It was simply that she couldn't be.

"It's not true," I whispered. "Mom was broken."

"How does that make you feel, Elle?" Kathy asked gently.

"Really sad."

"That is sad," Kathy agreed. "Sadness is a truth-based emotion, but there can be a false belief that causes us to hold onto it. Jesus wants to carry that for you. He wants to give joy and peace in trade for your sorrow. Are you willing to let go of it, or do you feel like you need to hold onto that sadness?"

"I want to let it go," I answered.

"See if you can gather up all that sadness as you think about your mom's brokenness, Elle. When you're ready, let me know and I'll pray."

I felt like I was digging up memory after memory. All the mom-wounds I felt as a child, even to the point that she checked into a mental health facility. I knew she hadn't meant to hurt me. But it still hurt. The tears flowed freely as I picked up each painful memory until my hands felt full.

"I'm ready."

"Jesus, will you carry this pain for Elle?"

Kathy asked the question simply. And then the pain was gone. Just gone. I couldn't explain it. It was gone. And in the stillness of the peace that washed over me, I heard these words: *I want to be your Friend.*

* * * * * * * *

Friend.

Just that one word and it all came rushing back.

Jesus.

When I was little, instead of an imaginary friend like most kids had, I imagined Jesus there with me all the time. The first time I thought of that was during vacation Bible school when I was five years old. VBS. I hadn't thought of that in years. My mom ran it. She did so much at the church. We were there early and stayed late. So strange, I hadn't remembered that my mom was strong at all, much less strong enough to organize and lead a program that reached hundreds of kids in our city. But it was there at VBS when I heard the story of Jesus talking with his disciples just before he went back up to heaven. He had said, *"I am with you always, even to the end of the age."*

I couldn't believe I still remembered that Bible verse. I determined to look it up later.

It had been my memory verse that week of VBS. I had repeated it over and over until it dawned on me that Jesus, even though he was going back to heaven, would be *with* his disciples, and he would be with me too.

The tears flowed freely now as the memories washed over

me. Scene after scene played out in my mind of times in my life. Me playing dolls alone in my room. Jesus was there. Me riding my bike, coasting down the big hill in front of my house, picking up speed as the wind whipped my hair straight back and my knuckles turned white on the handlebars. There was Jesus on the banana seat with me, his head thrown back laughing, his arms outstretched.

His arms outstretched.

And then as I grew older, dressing up to go out with my friends. Jesus was there, sitting nearby. But I had stopped talking to him. Stopped even noticing his presence.

When I was with Ethan, I didn't see Jesus there anymore. Funny, we had even talked about him briefly as we got to know each other. But at that point in my life, I never talked *to* him.

"What's going on in there, Elle?" Kathy asked gently. "Anything you want to share? Take your time if you're still processing."

I gulped down the lump in my throat and nodded, my eyes still closed as tears leaked out. "Jesus," I said, nodding in a way I hoped she understood. "He is there." I wiped my eyes with the Kleenex I had been clutching and pulled two more from the box. "He's always been there." I managed to get out the words before a fresh wave of tears broke loose.

My Jesus. My best friend. How had I left him aside for so many years? How could I have rejected him time and again for other people and other things as he sat there, watching, waiting?

"I'm so sorry," I whispered.

"What are you feeling, Elle?" Kathy asked.

"Ashamed," I answered.

"Why are you ashamed, Elle? What are you believing?"

I couldn't go to him. I had ignored him because if I paid attention, I would be required to live a certain way. I didn't want that. I didn't want his way. I wanted mine.

"I'm selfish."

"And what do you believe that means about you?" Kathy asked gently.

"I'm a bad person." I shook my head regretfully. The truth of that stung. In my own selfishness, I had turned my back on God. And all this time I had been believing he had turned his back on me. The shame and regret built like pressure in my sinuses as I fought to hold back my tears.

"What is the underlying belief there, Elle? If you're a bad person, that means what?"

The answer was obvious. "I'm no good," I whispered. "Worthless."

"Let yourself feel that, Elle. Does that feel true? Not *is* it true, but does it feel that way? See if your emotions confirm that."

I nodded, my eyes still closed. I felt that to my core. I felt like I was coated in black sooty ash, stained all over. It covered every part of me. Who could ever find worth in that mess?

"You're doing great, Elle," Kathy said. "Stay connected to your feelings. Are you willing to hear what God has to say about that? Can we ask Jesus if that's true?"

I nodded again.

"Jesus, what do you want Elle to know right there? She believes she is worthless. Is that true?"

Immediately, an image of a courtroom came to mind. I saw a shrouded judge, and instantly, I knew I was the one on trial. My accusers were everywhere — the voices in my head that had been telling me for so long how hopeless and bad I was. But then a figure stood up. A strong voice called out over the chaos.

She is worth everything to me!

It was Jesus. My Jesus. My best friend. The one I had rejected. The one I had pushed away for my own selfish desires. He was standing up for me.

I paid her debt.

Then I heard the judge's gavel hit the bench with an echoing thud.

She has been redeemed. Her penalty has been paid in full. The truth of the gospel came flooding back into my mind. My penalty was paid by Jesus. The Son of God himself gave his life in my place for the punishment my sins deserved.

I wanted to protest. How could he—why would he die for me? But in my mind's eye, I saw him. Jesus. Alive. Free. And in brilliant, gleaming light. His arms were outstretched, open, waiting for me.

The pressure that had built in my head burst into a flood of tears. And with my whole heart, I ran to him. And clung to him. The thought of his faithfulness overwhelmed me. The one who knew me best and loved me even through my worst.

My Jesus.

The love that washed over me in that moment changed everything. I couldn't really explain it or tell you what exactly changed, but I knew something had. And it affected everything. It was like color had returned to my world. I was loved. For no reason I could give. I was just simply loved. And I could receive it now. Freely and fully. Jesus loved *me*. This I knew.

Chapter 18

Following that one session with Kathy, I felt so different. Not a new Elle, per se, but the true Elle. I felt like I was just discovering who she really was. Who I really was. Not through the lens of my own pain, but through the eyes of God. Having his love gave me a whole new vantage point. I realized it acutely a few days later when I woke with a lightness in my heart.

"Good morning, Lord," I whispered sleepily. It was new for me. I just had to try it.

Good morning, child.

My heart leapt at the unbidden response that I felt or thought or . . . I couldn't quite figure out how to put it into words. My heart simply received the response I knew was from God's Spirit.

Tears filled my eyes. A response of joy mixed with wonder and humility at the idea that the God of the universe would speak to me.

"I want to live for you today, God," I whispered. "Will you show me how?"

Let's do it together.

I smiled. Jesus and me together. Just like the childhood

relationship I had with Jesus as my best friend. The imaginary friend that may or may not have come from my imagination. All I knew now was that he was real. He was talking to me.

"Thank you, Lord. Thank you for not giving up on me. Thank you for opening my eyes to all I was missing without you. I don't want to do anything without you ever again."

Then don't.

I wished it was that simple. I wished I could keep my own thoughts, my own will from taking over.

You can.

God was answering my thoughts now. Or was it me? I wasn't sure, but I kept going with it. "How?"

By my Spirit.

A Bible verse Miss Susie often quoted came to my mind. "Walk by the spirit . . ." But . . . how do I do that?

I stretched and rolled out of the bed. The brightening sky promised another sunny summer day. I pushed open the window above the small desk, and a symphony greeted my ears as birds trilled and chirped in lively staccatos and crescendos.

Breathing deeply of the peace and contentment that surrounded me, I opened my laptop. In the search bar, I typed the words I could remember of Miss Susie's verse.

Galatians 5:16 appeared. "So I say, walk by the Spirit, and you will not gratify the desires of the flesh."

Intrigued, I clicked open the Bible site and then a tab labeled 'Interlinear concordance.' It showed the verse in Greek and then in the King James Version. A memory popped into my mind. My dad, sitting at the kitchen table surrounded by books and Bibles. I remembered him showing me how to look up words in his big concordance to discover their original meaning. I was fascinated with the tiny text that filled the pages of that massive book. At nine years old, I felt like Indiana Jones unearthing hidden meanings. The memory left a warm feeling in my chest. It was the first happy memory of my dad I'd had in years. Funny how perspective can color an entire history.

I had let one rejection—albeit a life-altering one—negate a lifetime of love and nurturing my parents had given me. My chest panged at the realization. Did Dad think about me? Did he want to reconcile? My Heavenly Father did. He welcomed me with open arms. My earthly dad, with all his own issues that colored his perspective, wanted to follow God's example. I was certain of that. He was a man who wanted to walk by the Spirit.

I turned my focus back to the scripture. Scrolling through the Greek words, I located 'walk.'

"Peri-pa-te-o," I sounded out haltingly as I clicked on the Strong's Concordance entry G4043.

"Verb. To walk, to make one's way, progress; to make due use of opportunities." My eyes wandered through the definitions. "To live . . . follow as a companion . . . be occupied with."

Hmm. I smiled. Jesus and me, again. My companion. My best friend. Maybe to walk by the Spirit was as simple as just knowing my "imaginary" friend is right here with me all the time.

How could it be that all the time I was trying to outgrow my childish ways that was where I should have stayed all along?

"Lord, what do you want me to know about that?" I didn't know how to process everything like Kathy was coaching me, but I figured it didn't hurt to ask just in case I could hear an answer.

I waited, not hearing anything, but memories came rushing back. And Jesus was in them.

I tried to think through the next step of the process. Kathy called it MELT – memory, emotion. I had both of those. What was L? The lie. Was there a lie? There was certainly truth-based sadness. I had hurt my God who loved me. What was I to do with that?

I racked my brain trying to remember the process Kathy had explained. Oh, yeah. Could I let it go? Was there a reason I was holding onto that sadness? I stilled myself to examine the emotions. I knew I was forgiven. That felt true. I could let the sadness go.

"Lord, I give this over to you. I don't want anything to keep me from relationship with you now. Not ever again."

I felt the sadness lift, and peace washed in its place like a rolling wave smoothing back the eroding sand.

I'm here, Elle. I will never leave you. I never have.

* * * * * * * *

I felt almost silly gushing about the MELT process. I wanted to call all my college professors and even the mental health facility where I had interned. I did actually send the

CrossCounsel website link to my therapist back in Boston. Everyone should know about this. Most definitely the mental health facilities and educational programs.

Sharon tried to rein me in a bit after I had talked about it on the porch for the fifth night in a row. "Elle, I'm glad you experienced some breakthrough with this type of counseling," she said, "but I hope you can see that it is just a tool. You learned to use the tool. Not everyone learns to use it. I'm so glad it worked well for you, but it's not the only way that God brings people to freedom. We use it at Mercy House because emotions are pretty easy to connect with here, but for some people, they see breakthrough in other ways. God can use anything, and I'm glad he used this for you. But it is simply a tool. Don't make a god out of it."

I took her words to heart and tamped down my enthusiasm a bit. But when Kathy checked in with me again, I was ready to book another appointment.

* * * * * * *

Sharon closed the door behind her, and to my surprise, came to sit next to me on the sofa. I straightened, sensing something was wrong.

She cleared her throat. "Elle, I'm not sure how to tell you this . . . There is no easy way. I know how close you are to Rae."

My gut wrenched.

"Someone discovered drugs in her belongings."

I felt the blood drain from my face. In its place came a tidal wave of emotion.

Betrayal.

Guilt.

Remorse.

Fear.

Anger.

The inner turmoil escaped my lips as a painful wail, and I doubled over.

"Elle, I'm so sorry," I heard Sharon say as sobs shook my frame. "I know this must hurt you."

She had betrayed my trust. I was so angry at Rae, but angrier at myself. I was such an idiot. Such a liar. Such a hypocrite. These people trusted me, and I had betrayed their confidence. Then came Sharon's hand on my shoulder, like a calming, steady force. Slowly, I regained some composure and turned my tear-stained face to look her in the eye.

"I knew she was in trouble." I choked out the words. "I tried to protect her . . . protect Melvin. I failed. I'm so sorry."

Surprise, confusion, and then, slowly, an understanding look washed over Sharon's gently-lined face. My own face felt contorted in agony as I looked to her for something, some hope . . . mercy . . . but I knew I deserved to be fired. She said nothing but her eyes grew moist as she laid her hand on mine.

"What will happen to her? To Melvin?" The question laid heavy on my heart.

Silence suspended itself as I searched Sharon's eyes for an answer. She looked down at her hand resting on mine.

"It's a painful lesson," she said finally. "As much as we want to, we can't save everyone, Elle. People ultimately shoulder the responsibility for changing themselves."

With that, she gave my hand a pat and stood up.

Chapter 19

Tightening the laces of my running shoes, I eyed the gray sky. The air, thick with humidity, gave me pause about trying to run, but I had to get out of the house. I set out off the porch at a determined pace, stopping to open and close the pedestrian gate, and then continuing steadily down the long winding asphalt road. The clouds, heavy with rain, threatened a summer downpour as weighty as the grief that filled the house.

Rae and Melvin's departure cut deeply. She was sent directly back to the addiction recovery house, and Melvin was taken by CPS. Denise packed their belongings, and nothing more was said. Not about them. Not about my role in it. Yet, that didn't silence the grief. It was almost too much to bear. I could hardly focus on work. But surprisingly, instead of chastising me and saying, 'I told you so,' Denise told me to take the day off.

I had nowhere to go, of course, and certainly didn't feel like doing anything, so I went for a run, trying hard to avoid thinking, grasping at anything to keep grief from consuming me.

I hated rain. It caused my hair to frizz and inflate—not in a nice, full-bodied curly-girl look, but with awkward, wayward, flips and angles that resembled a cartoon character holding a key in an electrical socket. Sometimes, even the humidity had that effect, which is why I liked hats. Boston humidity was no joke, but this combination of intense Texas heat combined with damp air created a dankness you could cut with a knife. Thankfully, my hair was pulled back in a ponytail and looped through the hole at the back of my Red Sox cap.

Large water droplets began hitting the asphalt. Then the bill of my hat. My bare arms. The rain started slowly, then steadily quickened until a roar of hurling drops pelted the earth. Within moments, what had sounded like someone typing on a keyboard changed to the sound of a stadium of fans drumming on bleachers.

I ran faster. And faster. The rain increased against me, drenching me from head to toe. My feet slapped the wet pavement with ferocity. Exhausted, I slowed to a stop and doubled over, gulping for air.

Removing my hat, I lifted my head defiantly as the rain pelted my face. "It's not supposed to be this way!" I shouted to the sky.

"Cry out to him . . . Give him the chance to respond." Miss Susie's advice echoed in my brain.

"Why, God! Why??" I shouted into the rain. "Why do you let such awful things happen to people who are trying to live for you?"

I remembered Miss Susie's response.

"This life is not about our comfort or our pleasure—it's to bring

more people into the Kingdom of God before this life is over."

Why would anyone want to have any part of that if this is what it's like?

I thought of my dad. I didn't remember many of his sermons, but I clearly remembered a conversation we had in the little white church. I was thirteen, sitting in the back row. It was our last Sunday there. Dad and I were the only ones left in the building. He was gathering his things to leave, but he stopped and sat down beside me. I knew he was being forced out. And I knew it was about Mom. Because of her mental condition. Something about his inability to keep his own house in order so he couldn't lead a church. It hurt. It made me angry. Angry at the church people. Angry at my mom. Angry at God. I remembered asking Dad almost the same question.

"Why would anyone want to be a Christian if this is how you get treated?"

There was pain in his eyes as he put his arm around me and looked up at the altar where a large wooden cross hung against the backdrop.

"In this world we will have trouble," he quoted. "But take heart, I have overcome the world." He paused and looked at me. "Jesus said that, Elle. He said that after he had preached the good news that the Kingdom of God is here. That's pretty telling that the Kingdom of God isn't about living in peace and tranquility. It's about being with the King."

His words echoed in my mind.

The Kingdom of God isn't about living in peace and tranquility.

It's about being with the King.

I knew God was speaking to me.

Just be with me, Elle.

The whisper came to my heart as the rain slowed, gently mixing with my tears.

"Why does it have to be so hard?" I whispered back.

I didn't want it this way, child. I didn't want my children to experience pain and hardship. I desire for all things to be made right, and I made a way through my son Jesus.

"But it hurts now," I cried. "It hurts so bad."

You're not meant to go through this alone, Elle. I'm here. I'm grieving too. Take my hand. Let's walk through this together.

My Heavenly Father. My God, three-in-One. Father, Spirit, Son. The old Sunday school chorus rang in my head. He, that God, my God, he was grieving, too. And he wanted to be with me.

Jesus and me. As a child, I had imagined many times reaching for his scarred hand outstretched to me. When I was sad. When Mom flew into a rage. When Mom withdrew to a shrivel of the woman she had been. When we left the little church and Dad went to work in computer sales. When I tried to fit in with the kids at the new big church.

I've always been here for you, Elle. Through all of that. And I will carry you through it when it gets too hard.

"What about Rae?" I breathed shakily.

I'm here for her too. Don't stop loving her, Elle. Pray for her. There's power in your prayers.

* * * * * * *

If Miss Susie was surprised to see me, she didn't show it. When I followed Kiya into the prayer meeting, she invited me in as warmly as she did the rest of the girls. I took the Moms in Prayer sheet from her and settled myself into one of the folding chairs arranged in a circle. In my other hand was the old leather-bound Bible inscribed with my name.

Miss Susie rattled off the Bible verses each of us were to look up. Although once familiar with the order of the books of the Bible, I used the table of contents to find the book of Isaiah and rifled through the wispy pages until I found chapter 61. When it was my turn, I cleared my throat and read aloud, letting the words sink in and rest on me.

"The Spirit of the Sovereign Lord is upon me, for the Lord has anointed me to bring good news to the poor. He has sent me to comfort the brokenhearted and to proclaim that captives will be released and prisoners will be freed. He has sent me to tell those who mourn that the time of the Lord's favor has come, and with it, the day of God's anger against their enemies. To all who mourn in Israel, he will give a crown of beauty for ashes . . ." I paused as my voice cracked with emotion. "A joyous blessing instead of mourning, festive praise instead of despair. In their righteousness, they will be like great oaks that the Lord has planted for his own glory." I continued, reading the entire chapter, mesmerized by the words, even though the passage of focus was only the first three verses.

The readings continued, but I felt cocooned in my own little world, lifted, inspired, touched deeply by the words I'd read.

As Miss Susie began to pray, she reminded us of the power of our spoken words and encouraged us to speak out our praise to God.

"Lord, I praise you for being sovereign," Nikki said. "You rule over everything and nothing is beyond your control."

"Yes, Father God," Kiya added softly. "I praise you for overseeing all things."

I remained quiet, wishing the pounding of my heart would quiet down. I wanted to speak, but that familiar voice of fear kept me silent. As we entered into the time of silent confession, I eagerly confessed that fear to Jesus and asked him to forgive me for listening to it instead of him. And then, I took a deep breath . . . "Thank you, God, for this safe place to bring our burdens and lay them at your feet."

When Miss Susie explained again how to pray the scripture over the children, she prefaced it by saying we could pray for anyone we wanted to. I chose Melvin.

Uncertain, even timidly, I began reading the words on the page with Melvin's name inserted. "Father, I pray that, out of your glorious riches, you will strengthen Melvin with power through your Spirit in his inner being, so that Christ may dwell in Melvin's heart through faith."

Following suit with how the others had prayed, I

continued with my own requests for him, just like I would've wanted someone to pray for my own child. "Please protect him. Keep him safe physically, mentally, and emotionally." My mind flew with images of what he might be going through wherever he was. "Help him know you are with him always," I concluded, thinking of the verse that was imprinted on my heart and mind. "And help Rae know that, too. Amen."

When the prayer meeting was over, I felt better than I had the whole two weeks since Rae left. I hadn't realized the amount of worry I was carrying for her and Melvin. It felt good to give that over to God.

Thank you, Lord, I thought, slipping easily into my child-like awareness of his presence. *It feels good to know they are in your hands.*

Chapter 20

Slowly, things began to normalize around the house, but a damper of gloom still hung in the air. Musty and thick like dust in an unused room. Without light or life. I wondered how many times this old house had seen such times. Likely more than I wanted to know. The absence of Rae's wit and humor meant that laughter didn't come as easily. Fun just didn't feel the same. So, instead of "fun," I decided to lift the mood by planning a celebration of life for Judith's baby.

Denise stamped her approval on my idea—most likely due to Sharon's enthusiasm. At first, showing her true colors, she was against it. "Keeping emotion out of it is best for a client when they choose to give their baby up for adoption." Emotion is unavoidable, I pointed out. You either stuff it or you express it.

I had gotten better at standing my ground with her, but whenever I pushed too hard, she dug in her heels and insisted on her way or the highway, literally. In this case, though, I had strategically mentioned the idea when Sharon was nearby. She overheard and inserted her opinion, saying a celebration of life would help reinforce the value of new life among both the clients and those who attended.

So, when Denise conceded, I called Stephanie at Embrace Grace to help form a plan. She suggested a joint party with Judith and the adoptive parents, celebrating the baby and the roles both the birth mom and the adoptive mom would have in his life. Embrace Grace, a ministry that supported single mothers, would invite some of their supporters. Mercy House could invite our supporters, and together we would make a sweet celebration. I decided to involve all the girls in the preparations, even Judith herself. It provided a needed distraction as we set to work at the large kitchen table making collaged invitations and handmade decorations.

"You do know you can buy pre-made invitations at Hobby Lobby, right?" Serena asked, with more than a hint of complaining in her voice. "My fingers ain't made for this kind of work." She was attempting to drop a spot of glue on the back of a die-cut baby rattle tinier than her pinky nail.

"Isn't this more fun though?" I asked with a smile.

"If that's what you want to call it," Nikki said, puffing a wisp of long hair out of her face as she carefully cut out a paper decoration.

"I like it," Judith volunteered. "Sure beats studying."

Murmured agreements echoed around the little circle as the group concentrated on their tasks.

"I like the theme," Kiya offered quietly. "These decorations would probably fit the twins right now." She held up a miniature bassinet I had bought to hold notes of affirmation guests could write to Judith.

"That's so tiny!" Judith said. "The twins are that small?"

"Yeah, they are the size of small zucchinis," she said, smiling and rubbing her large abdomen.

"Can you even feel them?" Judith asked. "That's so different than this one. He's a cantaloupe."

All the women compared their progression against a colorful chart on the kitchen wall that showed the stage of baby development in comparison to fruit. The two girls looked to be at almost the same stage of pregnancy, but Judith was well into her third trimester, while Kiya was just nearing the end of her second.

"I feel them all the time," Kiya laughed. "A sharp little foot or something keeps digging at my ribs."

"I don't know how you're going to handle two babies," Nikki said, shaking her head. "Can you imagine if there were two Allanna's around here?"

We all laughed knowingly. Little Allanna, as cute as she was, certainly was a handful.

A flicker of sadness shadowed Kiya's face, but her gentle smile returned quickly. No doubt she was thinking of Thomas and his absence.

I wondered if anyone could handle twins as a single mom, but I knew she had support. Since things had broken off with the baby daddy, her relationship with her mom had improved greatly.

"I'll manage," she said. "I think twins can be best of friends, so maybe they will entertain each other."

Definitely wishful thinking for the infancy stage, I was certain, but no one pressed the issue.

We worked quietly for a few moments until Babs broke the silence.

"I ain't never been to a baby party," she said. She held up a long piece of ribbon and snipped it to the length of a bow. "What's it like?"

"It's basically a shower," Serena said nonchalantly, carefully creasing the fold of an invitation she'd just finished.

This celebration wasn't meant to be a typical baby shower. Stephanie and I agreed it would be too hard for Judith to see baby items being unwrapped. I had mentioned that to the girls when Judith wasn't present, and I hoped they would be sensitive in talking about it.

"A shower?" Babs's face contorted into a question mark.

"Pretty much," Serena said without looking up from her work.

"How's that a party?" Babs asked.

"It's not meant to be a party," I interjected.

"Right. That's why I said shower," Serena repeated.

"Surely you don't mean a real shower," Babs said.

"Which is why I said, it's basically a shower," Serena said with annoyance.

I looked up from my work just as Babs caught my eye. Her eyes were wide with concern.

"What?" I asked. The word was out of my mouth before it dawned on me that she probably thought the word "shower" shouldn't be mentioned in front of Judith. And she would've been right. But it was done.

"It's not a typical shower," I said quickly, trying to cover Serena's gaff before Judith became concerned. "Most showers would make a show of the unwrapping part, but this will be different. We won't have gifts. There won't be dressing games or any games, for that matter." They looked at me blankly. Had they never had to play the torturous game of putting clothes on a baby doll? "You know the whole dressing and undressing game?" I waved off the explanation and continued. "Instead, we will have finger foods, light beverages, and those who aren't shy can stand up in front of everyone to say a few words."

Stephanie had come up with all that. I had also suggested we ask a few people to pray for both moms, but I didn't mention that now.

"So, mostly like a shower," Serena said.

Apparently, she didn't get the idea that I was trying to play down the comparison to a baby shower. The anticipation and joy those brought were a far cry from what Judith would experience.

I knew she would never intentionally make Judith feel badly, but she remained bent over her tasks, not even looking up to see the 'shut it' signal I wanted to give her.

Babs shook her head no, muttering 'nuh-uh' under her breath. She got it.

But Serena continued with a giggle. "Shower games are so awkward. Especially when guys are involved. You ever been to a shower with guys?"

I was about to cut her off bluntly, but Babs beat me to it.

"That's it—I can't handle this. Yall's outta yo minds!"

All heads turned to her quizzically. She slammed the scissors on the table and threw both hands on her ample hips. "Undressin' and showerin' in a group? Standing up in front of everybody—even guys? Yall's crazy!"

It took a moment to register her confusion before we burst out laughing at the Amelia-Bedelia moment. Of course, Babs had no context for what a baby shower was. She'd never even heard of one until now.

I had doubted we would be able to laugh at all, but here we were. Laughter filled Mercy House once again.

Chapter 21

A sharp rap on my door startled me awake. Sharon didn't even wait for me to get out of bed but opened the door. "Kiya's in trouble. Contractions. Early labor."

Way early labor. I threw back the cover. She was only twenty-eight weeks along.

"I've called an ambulance," Sharon said matter-of-factly.

My gut wrenched.

"Get Denise on the phone. Have her coordinate help here at the house. I'll go in the ambulance with Ki. You meet us there." She looked at me pointedly before closing the door. "She needs you, Elle."

I jumped into my joggers and grabbed a hoodie, pulling a beanie over my unbrushed hair before heading out the door.

I was outside when the paramedics carried Kiya out on a stretcher. She was crying quietly, whether in pain or fear, I wasn't sure. My heart was in my throat. With no words of assurance to offer, I reached for her hand and clutched it briefly as they loaded her into the ambulance. And then I hurried to the van.

This time, the trek through the hospital corridors didn't

faze me. My thoughts were only on Ki and the twins. I needed to get to her. She needed me.

"Elle," Sharon called as I passed the waiting room. "They aren't letting anyone in. We just need to wait here. You can contact the prayer partners."

"I already did." I had done that from the van while waiting to follow the ambulance. In a separate message to Miss Susie, I added a few extra details, including a hurried, "Pray that I can be a help to her."

The hours dragged on as we sat there. Sharon fell asleep in the chair, waiting. I couldn't. Restlessly, I flipped through magazines, checking my phone for anything that might help pass the time and distract my worries. In my haste, I hadn't thought to bring my computer. Desperate for something to console my thoughts, I picked up the Bible on the end table in the waiting room and began reading in the book of John.

In the beginning was the Word, and the Word was with God, and the Word was God. He was with God in the beginning. Through him all things were made; without him nothing was made that has been made. In him was life, and that life was the light of all mankind. The light shines in the darkness, and the darkness has not overcome it.

The words, beautiful and strong, settled my heart. I continued reading, fascinated by the descriptions and actions of Jesus, particularly the conversation he had with Nicodemus. I was struck by his words, "Truly, truly, I say to you, unless one is born of water and the Spirit he cannot enter into the kingdom of God." Born of water as in physical birth, and born spiritually as well. How many times had I heard my father talk about being 'born again,' yet the words melded in with other 'Christianese' phrases and became white noise I never sought to understand. But here, in the Scriptures, it was clear to me now. Rebirth. Born again, into a holy Kingdom, which I now knew was a very real realm where God resided. Right here. In our midst.

I read on until I was stopped at the familiar Bible verse I had received a gold star for memorizing as a child. John 3:16. *For God so loved the world that he gave his one and only Son, that whoever believes in him shall not perish but have eternal life.*

I paused and pondered the words, vaguely recalling a lifetime of explanations:

God had a job that could only be accomplished through Jesus . . . He sent Jesus on a mission from heaven to make a way for people to be brought back into God's family, and Jesus saw it through . . . Jesus accomplished his work on the cross when he died for the sins of mankind, and now those who have been born again by the Spirit, their spirits live on even after their physical bodies die.

But death still hurts, Lord. It hurts terribly for those who lose someone. "Please, please don't let Ki lose the twins. Please save them, God."

I blinked away tears to focus on the blurry words.

For God did not send his Son into the world to condemn the world, but to save the world through him.

I read it again. I had never known these words followed the most famous verse in the Bible. *For God did not send his*

Son into the world to condemn the world, but to save the world through him.

Miss Susie was right. God wasn't waiting to punish people because they stepped out of line. He sent Jesus to save them.

My heart leapt. Was God speaking to me? Did he mean that Kiya wouldn't be judged for her past? Of course he did! So then . . . I caught my breath. Was he telling me the babies would be saved?

Adrenaline raced through me. I snapped the Bible shut and jumped to my feet, pacing back and forth quickly across the room.

"Elle?" Sharon lifted her head, blinking the sleep from her eyes. "Did something happen?"

Before I could explain my thoughts, the door opened and a doctor in surgical scrubs entered the room.

Sharon stood.

I held my breath.

The doctor wasn't smiling. She looked grave.

"Kiya?" Sharon asked.

"She is stable," the doctor replied. "She lost a lot of blood, but she's going to be fine. It will be a little while before the sedation wears off, but you are welcome to sit in the recovery room to wait for her to wake."

The doctor paused.

"The babies?" Sharon pressed.

"A girl and a boy. They were in distress. Kiya's daughter has been taken to the neo-natal intensive care unit. It will be touch and go for a while, but she's in good hands. Her son," she paused again. "I'm sorry to inform you that her son did not survive."

Chapter 22

With a brief, sympathetic touch on my arm, Sharon left to go to Kiya in the recovery room.

I collapsed on the waiting room bench, shaken. It felt like I had been gut-punched. Breath knocked out of me. Again.

It seemed surreal. Unbelievable. How could God let this happen?

Kiya, her quiet, gentle spirit, already so broken by the circumstances of her young life. How would she cope?

Why? Why? God! Why?

Those were the only words rattling in my brain as the deep crushing pain of losing my own baby swept in like a powerful undertow. I felt myself going numb in response, retreating into the condition I had known before Mercy House. I gasped for breath. Everything was being sucked out of me, threatening to leave me with nothing. No emotion. No hope. No life. A black wall of nothingness loomed before me.

Ki needed me now more than ever, yet I had nothing to give her. I wanted words of comfort. Words of hope. Words from God. But I had none of that. Instead, just another crushing blow from life. Where was God in this?

I grasped at the last straw—a desperate wish of a prayer, hoping God would answer.

"Are you even here, God?"

Nothing.

Just a big silent void of nothingness.

How did I get duped by faith again?

But God promised to be with me always, I argued with myself, remembering Matthew 28:20.

Then where is he? My cynical thoughts taunted me. *Why can't I feel him? Why can't I hear him? And why does he keep allowing tragedy after tragedy?*

"Where are you, God?" I whispered. "We need you now. I need you so I can help Kiya."

The door to the waiting room opened. Denise. I looked at her, sure my face said it all. But I choked out the words. "One of the babies . . . died."

She nodded. "I know."

Tears sprang to my eyes. Of all people to cry in front of . . . But I couldn't hold them back. I was afraid to hold them back, afraid doing so would push me over the cliff of nothingness.

"I guess you're going to tell me I shouldn't let my heart get involved," I said, swiping at the tears that flowed freely.

Denise said nothing. She sat down beside me, hands clasped in her lap, back straight, poised. Of course.

I hung my head, the pain of what happened searing into me. "I don't understand God," I whispered through my tears. "He could have stopped this. He could have made it all right. Kiya has already been through so much. Why would he allow this?"

Denise stayed silent. I couldn't. I had to let it out. It was my only way of coming up for air beneath the suffocating waves.

"I was so sure God was going to save them . . ." I admitted hoarsely. "I thought I was finally at the place where I could hear him. I have been told over and over about how God wants to have a personal relationship with me. So I put myself out there. I was praying, reading the Bible. And I thought he gave me a verse. You know how Sharon says sometimes a verse just jumps off the page? That's what happened. I thought he was finally confirming my faith." I shook my head, the tears cutting streams down my cheeks. "How do I know that anything I believe is even real? I just don't understand him," I whispered.

Denise cleared her throat. "Scripture—God's Word—must be handled carefully," she said matter-of-factly. "Anyone can manipulate it with their own thoughts. Satan took God's words and put his spin on them in the desert with Jesus. Understanding Scripture accurately requires diligent study . . . and prayer."

I turned my back to her, pulling my hood over my beanie, hoping she would just leave me to my own thoughts. I didn't need to deal with her on top of everything else.

"Hard things have a way of defining you," she continued, impervious to my body language. "No matter how much you wish life could be pain-free, hard things build your faith. There's a scripture in John 15 about that. Jesus told his disciples, 'I am the true vine, and my Father is the gardener. He cuts off every branch in me that bears no fruit, while every branch that does bear fruit he prunes so that it will be even more fruitful.' Being pruned sure isn't pleasant. It's painful. But it's necessary for growth."

I remained silent with my back to her, hoping that would end her soliloquy. But it didn't.

"He goes on to say, 'I am the vine; you are the branches. If you remain in me and I in you, you will bear much fruit; apart from me you can do nothing.'"

I was slightly impressed she could quote so much of the Bible. She had never spoken to me about faith, and from her attitude toward me, I had judged her in a different category than Miss Susie and Sharon and Kathy. Still, the words she chose to quote sure didn't bring me comfort. Maybe she was right about the devil taking God's words and putting his own spin on them.

Denise cleared her throat again, and I couldn't help rolling my eyes, glad my back was still toward her. Now what? Where else could she kick me while I was down? What kind of instruction did she have to make Elle a better person? I braced myself.

"I'm a pretty private person. Don't talk much about my own woes. But I've had plenty. Mostly brought on by myself. My ways. What some would call a control issue."

A scoff escaped my lips, and I turned in my seat to look at her. Surely she said that tongue-in-cheek. Of course she had a control issue. What else could it be called?

Denise was still looking straight ahead, unsmiling. No

sign of joking. Not that I would expect her to ever joke. Her face was somber and she briefly dipped her head to look at her hands. I coughed to disguise my reaction, and then waited for her to continue.

"I don't tell many people this," she said, "but I was Sharon's first client."

Chapter 23

The significance of Denise's words dawned slowly on me.

"Got pregnant and Sharon showed me mercy even before a Mercy House existed," she stated matter-of-factly.

Wide-eyed, I gaped at her profile. Was this stoic, impenetrable force of a woman actually being vulnerable with me?

"It was a lot more taboo in those days to be pregnant out of wedlock. I had shamed my family. My own mother made me leave the house. Wanted me to marry the kid who got me pregnant, but it would never have worked. We were both too immature. I was just eighteen. Headstrong. No one could tell me what to do."

She stared straight ahead as if she had spoken to the door instead of me. Her mouth pursed thoughtfully, and then she continued. "Sharon and Rick took me in. Tried to help me. But I had issues accepting help from anybody. It was the worst thing I could imagine—having to lean on other people. To my immature mind, it was a sign of weakness, and I was too proud to show any weakness. Too proud . . ."

Her voice trailed off, and I held my breath, afraid the spell would be broken.

Denise shook her head slowly. "I wasn't thinking straight. Thought I could fix things, and move on. I thought I could put it all behind me. Thought an abortion would free up my future. Instead, it dictated it. Because I have regretted it every . . . single . . . day."

She swallowed hard, and from the side view, I could see liquid fill her eyes. The weight of what she was saying settled on my shoulders like a dark gloom.

"Why are you here now?" I asked, quietly. But I knew the answer. It was the same reason I was here. Partly to punish herself and partly to find solace, or pay penance, by helping others.

"After the guilt set in, I came crawling back to Sharon. Begged her to let me help her. I needed a purpose. A reason to go on."

Exactly.

"She did help me, more than I dreamed. Helped me find God in a way I hadn't known him before. It was then that John 15 became so real to me. I had a choice. I could surrender my own plans and dreams and plug into the Vine or go my own way apart from God. The interesting thing about a branch is that it doesn't have control over how the vine grows. It produces fruit by just being connected to the vine. I knew God was asking me to give control of my life over to him." She cleared her throat. "Being a take-charge person isn't a bad thing. It's good when it's used in the right way. But my need for control had become like a wild shoot strangling anything it could grab onto. If I remained connected to the Vine, I would be pruned because God wanted me to bear fruit. And I needed a lot of pruning. Still do."

Mhmm.

She paused and turned to look at me, making me wonder if I had affirmed that aloud.

"Growth always comes through suffering if we stay connected to the Vine." Her eyes pointedly met mine. "God always works even the bad circumstances together for our good. He never wastes pain."

My eyes filled with fresh tears as I thought about my baby. And now Kiya's infant son. This was basically the same thing Miss Susie had said about my baby, but I couldn't imagine what good could come from that.

"Did he have to take a child's life to teach a lesson?" I whispered.

"It's not about teaching lessons, Elle," Denise said sharply. "That's not how God works. There will always be bad things in this world, with or without God. It's about staying connected to him through it all. He's our source, he's our strength, he's our sustainer. Without him, we are useless. He will take care of you. He will take care of Kiya. The pruning is part of that care, and no, losing a child is not his way of pruning. What he will prune is how you relate to him—the way you think of him, the ideas you have about him that keep you from living in the fullness he wants for you."

I wanted to believe that. I did. But—

"But it's so unfair," I burst out. "No one deserves to feel the pain of losing their child."

Denise turned again to face the closed door, refusing to look at my pained face that begged for answers. Her dark eyes stared forward, deep in thought, while I painfully waited for an answer. A reason. Anything.

"Fair," she mused quietly. "I learned a long time ago that 'fair' isn't in God's dictionary. Instead, it reads 'justice' and 'mercy.'"

Her words surprised me. And confused me.

She continued. "Not one of us deserve anything good, Elle. Not one. We deserve punishment. The Bible tells us that in black and white. It all started right there in the garden of Eden with sin. The penalty for sin is death. So if you want to talk about fair, you only have to think as far as Jesus. Was it fair for him to die for your sin or mine? But God chose mercy. He wanted to save you. He wanted to save me. And he had to do it through justice, which meant that penalty had to be paid."

"What does any of that have to do with what Ki is dealing with right now?" I questioned, frustrated.

"Everything," Denise retorted. "It has everything to do with it. Pain is inescapable in this world. Even the pain of losing a child."

I doubled over in my seat, my emotions turning into a searing physical ache. "How can someone recover from that kind of pain?" I moaned.

We sat in silence, each feeling the weight of grief we carried. Little by little, the searing calmed to the old, dull ache I had become accustomed to. The minutes ticked by, and I wondered why we were waiting here. What was there to do? What was the point? What was the point in anything? I had nothing to say to Kiya. I couldn't bear to see her.

After a long while, Denise spoke.

"The way I see it," she said slowly, "there are two ways to deal with pain. You can let it eat you up, or you can let God use it somehow."

I remained silent for a moment, considering her words. "Some people probably allow both," I said.

"Maybe," she acknowledged.

"What have you done with your pain?" I asked tentatively.

Denise's profile remained steady, staring at the closed door. "I like to think God is using it for good at Mercy House."

You're also letting it eat you up, I wanted to say. I could see now that she hung onto pain as a way to punish herself. It explained a lot about her attitude. My thoughts remained unspoken. Instead, I said something Miss Susie told me once.

"You know, I heard someone say once that Jesus's sacrifice on the cross forgave the debt of sin once and for all."

"That's true," she affirmed. "It's in the book of Hebrews."

"So," I said softly, half musing to myself, "if we keep punishing ourselves, isn't that like saying Christ's sacrifice wasn't enough?"

Denise's full bottom lip trembled slightly. I looked away.

We sat in silence side by side, two very different individuals, strangely connected by pain.

After several minutes had passed, I broke the silence.

"Do you think God's pruning helped your control issues?" I asked.

"Hmph," Denise grunted. "Oh, I know it did." She paused and looked at me from the corner of her eye without ever turning toward me. "Sometimes the bad stuff has a way of growing back though, and needs regular trimming . . . I suppose you think I try to control you?"

I merely shrugged. Of course that's what I thought, but I didn't want to get anything started. I preferred this vulnerable Denise and certainly didn't want to engage her in battle.

"I still have more to learn in that area," she said. "But I have learned that my way isn't always right. So, I do give in a little easier now."

I would've laughed, but didn't feel like it.

"And I've learned to give credit where credit is due," she added. "I do admit, your way of doing things has done a lot of good. There's a different feeling in the house. You have brought a certain joy to the place."

Wait. Was she actually saying something nice about me? I turned to her with a slight smirk. "So, you're telling me you were wrong and I was right?"

Denise set her lips and turned her face back toward the waiting room door. I held my breath, wondering if the moment had passed. What I had thought might be a fissure in the ice seemed to freeze back over in the silence that followed. How dumb to try drawing humanity out of this woman. She couldn't even take a playful tease.

Then Denise muttered. "All I'm telling you is that there's more than one way to handle things."

I thought I saw a smile playing at her lips, as she slid her eyes toward me. "And you do resemble a pair of pruning shears."

Chapter 24

Kiya remained at the hospital several days after baby Tessia was born. I only saw her once during that time. It was right before the memorial service for her son, whom she named Theodore. I took a fresh bag of clothes to her in the NICU, including an outfit for the memorial service. In the bag, I also included a small, soft teddy bear. Kiya came out to meet me in the waiting room. Her eyes looked dull and hollow. Like she wasn't even there.

We said nothing. I still had no words to offer but embraced her in a firm hug that was only half-heartedly returned. I pressed the bag into her hand, hoping my eyes conveyed my apologies. I would not be going to the memorial service. We parted ways then, and I headed back down the long corridor.

* * * * * * * *

One afternoon, when my duties were done for the day, I retreated to my bedroom, physically and emotionally drained. Even though I continued my morning runs, the level of stress kept me physically exhausted. I had just lain down on my bed, when I heard a light rap on the door. Begrudgingly, I heaved myself up to answer it. Miss Susie's small, round shape greeted me. She hadn't been up the stairs at Mercy House the entire time I'd been there, so I was curious what caused her to make the climb. No doubt, it was an effort.

"Hi, darlin'," she said, only slightly winded. "I was just dropping by a casserole I made. Just a little something in anticipation of Kiya's return. I know you girls will be running up to the NICU every day till little Tessia comes home."

"That's very thoughtful, Miss Susie. Thank you," I said, still surprised that she would come all the way up here to tell me that.

"I wanted to check on you, too," she said in answer to my unspoken question. "I know you've been carrying a lot. Is there anything I can pray with you about?"

Unwilled tears filled my eyes. Why did Miss Susie always elicit this response??

I motioned her inside and closed the door.

I swiped away the tears and perched on the edge of my bed. Miss Susie came near and gently laid her warm, round hand on my shoulder.

"How can I pray for you, darlin'?"

I merely shrugged, and then muttered, "That I won't be such a screwup friend."

"Elle, honey," Miss Susie said, "you are not a screwup."

"You don't know." I shook my head, hoping to shake away

the truth, but it was right there. "I was a terrible friend to Rae. I could have stopped her. I could have made her come clean with Denise and Sharon about what was going on. But I was weak. I thought I was helping, but I made it so much worse. And then Ki needed me. She needs me now. But I can't even be there for her in her hardest moments. I'm just so weak. A horrible friend."

The words tumbled out with such ease, I could have continued on and on, but Miss Susie stopped me.

"That's a lie," she said fiercely. "Don't you take that on. That is a lie straight from the pit of hell."

Her eyes bore into mine as she lifted my chin.

"You are strong, Elle. You have come here to help these women, and you are helping them. You helped Rae in a way that you won't know this side of heaven. And you have helped Kiya already, too. But you're not done. There's so much more to you. So much more to offer."

"I can't. I don't . . ." I shook my chin from her grasp as the tears came freely. "I have nothing left to give. Anything good I've ever had is gone."

I thought of my baby, Ethan, my mom and dad, and the happy family we once had.

"I'm empty, Miss Susie. I have nothing left."

The little round lady before me placed her hands on her hips. I supposed she was silently surveying what a mess I was. She grimly shook her head.

"Now that's a fine pity puddle you're getting real comfortable in, isn't it?"

I frowned at her through my tears.

"Elle, honey, you might be tempted to think God hasn't been good to you, but the truth is, no matter how you feel or what you think, blessing is not the absence of hard things. It is Christ's presence in the midst of it all. Anything that makes you need God is a blessing. It's an opportunity to know him better. What have you learned about him through your loss? And what can you teach others about him now?"

I looked at her skeptically.

"God will give you beauty for ashes, just like the scripture says, if you let him."

The words she spoke resonated inside me. I thought of what Denise had said about letting God use our pain, and I remembered the scripture as the one I had read in Moms in Prayer. I knew what she said was true. Somehow, I just knew it was.

"As long as you have life, you have hope, Elle," Miss Susie continued. "Look for it. And give it away to someone who needs it now. Faith, hope, and love will always remain. Find where they are bottled up inside you and pour them out to a hurting world that needs them. Don't keep them locked up, honey. You have people around you who may only receive them from you."

My voice trembled as I squeaked out the question on my heart. "How?" I wanted to know. More than ever, I wanted to know.

"You'll figure that out when you get in the presence of Jesus. Spend some time asking him that question."

She grasped both of my hands in hers and prayed, "Father, Elle is seeking answers and your Word says that if we seek, we will find. Would you show Elle the answers she needs from you? Show her the hope you have placed inside her to share with others. And give her strength, Lord, to do just what you're asking her to do."

She dropped my hands and then lifted her chubby forefinger to point to me. "Now, it's your turn. You keep praying. He is here. Talk to him, Elle."

She turned on her heel and left the room, clicking the door shut behind her. I remained staring at the door for a moment, wondering what to do next.

Finally, I lifted myself from where I had been leaning against the bed. Slowly, I turned and knelt. It was the way I had learned to talk to God from an early age. Side by side with my mom. My mind flashed with a memory of her leading me in prayer as we talked to God together. There were so many sweet memories I had of my mama. Daddy too. I had been focusing only on the negative. I learned a lot from both of them. They loved me. The truth of that settled on my heart, and somehow it didn't feel like a loss. I still had their love. I still had their teaching. I had been shaped by them.

Love remained. Miss Susie was right. No mistakes, no circumstances, not even death could take it away.

It's the same with Baby Claire.

The thought came like a knife to my heart.

Baby Claire.

It was the name Ethan and I had chosen after we came to terms with the pregnancy. I hadn't thought about her name since that awful day at the hospital when I had left empty. Empty womb. Empty arms. Empty heart. Though I grieved deeply, I had tried desperately to keep her nameless, hoping that somehow that would ease the pain. But at each milestone, her little form came to mind. January 12th, her due date. The date Ethan had given me the little box I never opened.

Would she have been wrinkled and red? Would she resemble Ethan or me more? I could see her little form, but never a face. Even as I had watched little Melvin grow, I could imagine her chubby legs, tiny toes, hair forming on her little round head, curling slightly at the back. But I still couldn't see her face. I could never see her face.

The thoughts swirled around me, engulfing me. This is why I never allowed myself to think too much about her.

"Oh, God!" I cried in a muted whisper. "It hurts."

But love remains.

The thought came like a still, steadying force, lifting me from the swirling floodwaters.

Love.

It was true. The love I had for her was different than any I had ever known. I still had it, though it pained me greatly now.

Grief is love that can no longer be given away.

I had read that somewhere in the many books I had consumed in the darkest months after losing her.

You have so much to give.

The sentiment Miss Susie offered echoed in my mind. I had love bottled up in me that I needed to share. I needed to let it out. But I longed to give it all to Baby Claire.

She will always be a part of you. She has helped make you into the woman you are today.

Somehow that thought brought a deep sense of peace that washed over me, much like the freedom I had received in the session with Kathy. I knew it was truth. Baby Claire had touched my life deeply, maybe deeper than anyone so far, because my love for her was so very great. Her little baby fingerprints were now all over my heart. God had used her to help shape me into the person I was becoming. In many ways, her life, though so very brief, had saved mine.

"Father," I began slowly, my head bowed against the mattress, "thank you for Baby Claire." My voice broke as her name passed across my lips. "She was your gift to me. She woke me up to a love I had never known before. The love of a parent for a child. A glimpse of your love for your children. Thank you, God, for my precious baby. Thank you for the privilege of having had her in my life. I have learned so much, changed so much, because of her. Thank you for using her to reach my heart. I am forever grateful. Her life had great purpose, and I don't want that purpose to end with me. Give me strength, give me courage, Father, to tell about what you've done through her. Please show me how you want me to share the love that remains. Amen."

Chapter 25

Kiya entered the kitchen, slowly and deliberately, having forced herself out of her bed at Sharon's prodding. She had missed breakfast for the third time in a row since returning to the house, and Sharon had insisted she come downstairs to eat something. She was not taking care of herself. Not eating right, not drinking as much as she should. Her hair looked like it hadn't been washed in weeks. Making daily trips to the NICU to feed Tessia, she looked haggard and worn despite her youth. Her presence carried the same dull, lifelessness that I had sensed right after her C-section. Previously soft, kind eyes that had been quick to offer a smile were now hollow. Expressionless.

My heart ached for her, and its pace quickened as I thought about what to say.

The large kitchen was empty, except for the two of us. The other girls were in class, and Denise was in our shared office. The silence was palpable, save for the noise of whirring thoughts in my brain, as I considered ways to speak to her. I had tried many times before to come up with the right words to say, but each time, silence, fear, and avoidance had won out. This time, I determined to push through. No words could help, I knew, but spurred on by the idea of sharing the love that remained, I set to work, reheating her breakfast.

Wordlessly, I laid a placemat on the table in front of her and set it with a napkin and utensils. Remembering Sharon's instructions that she must drink plenty to increase her milk supply for baby Tessia, I poured her a large glass of water. I chose a pretty juice glass and filled it with apple juice. Finally, retrieving the plate from the microwave, I placed it before her and sat down.

Kiya stared straight ahead, leaving the items untouched, and I wondered if she knew I was there.

Taking a cue from Miss Susie, I reached for her hand and awkwardly, stiltedly, I prayed. "Father, thank you. Thanks for this food. Please . . ." I faltered, not quite knowing what to pray as my mind grasped for words. "Would you please use it to nourish Ki so that she can nourish little Tessia? And could you . . . I mean, would you bless that baby and help her to come home soon? Amen." The end rattled off a little too quickly, but I breathed a sigh of relief and looked at Kiya.

Her eyes blinked. "Thank you," she said, her voice monotone.

She didn't reach for the food.

"Ki, you should eat," I said gently.

She picked up her fork and proceeded to push the food around the plate aimlessly.

My eyes filled with tears. I saw myself in her. I had been where she was now. It was painful to see someone wasting away before you, and it gave me new empathy for Ethan.

I felt helpless.

"Kiya," I said tenderly, leaning toward her, willing her to look at me. "I know there are no words that can help you right now, but I want you to know I'm here for you. My heart is hurting for you . . . " I swallowed hard. "And with you."

She looked at me then, her eyes starting to brim with tears. Her eyes searched mine, and I saw a flash of desperation. Her bottom lip quivered, and slowly she squeaked out a single word. "Why?"

Fear seized my heart as I watched the tears brim over and roll down her cheeks. She was asking me why. Me! The one who had the very same questions!

"Why did God let this happen?" she asked, her voice cracking and trailing off to a sob.

My mind raced, frantically trying to call forth something that well-wishers had told me.

"I don't know that God let it happen," I offered lamely.

"But he did," she said, her voice now passionate. She was right. He could've stopped it. It was the same question that never was satisfactorily answered for me.

"He sees the bigger picture," I tried again, grasping at something Miss Susie had said. "And even though not everything goes like we hope it will, he works it all together for good in the end."

"But why would God think it's better for a baby to be born and die than to never have lived at all?" Her voice trailed off in angry sobs. And her head bowed as the tears fell into her napkin.

A huge lump filled my throat. I could not speak. My sinuses filled with unshed tears. Then suddenly, I knew the answer. It had been stuck there in my heart the whole time. Thoughts of Baby Claire filled my head. The rush of feeling when I heard her heartbeat for the very first time. Me watching and waiting for my abdomen to swell ever so slightly. The faint flutter of life I felt within me. Ethan gently laying his head on my tummy, whispering love to her.

I don't know how long had passed before the lump eased, but when it did, I knew it was time to share Baby Claire, to tell what a difference her brief life had made . . . and to allow it to make a difference in another's.

"Not many people know this," I began hoarsely, "but I lost a baby too."

Ki looked up at me. She reached for my hand and clutched it fiercely.

The pressure that had built in my sinuses erupted. My eyes overflowed with tears and my body began to shake with sobs.

Kiya reached for me and embraced me. Together, we grieved for our babies, both of us sobbing with the deep sorrow that death brings. As the sobs slowed, I recalled the words, *Love remains.*

"Ki," I said, drawing back to look into her grieving eyes, "your son's life is so valuable. It didn't end with death. I can picture him now in the arms of Jesus with my baby, too. His life here on earth may have been brief, but it was so impactful.

He impacted me and everyone else in this house, too. God knew it was much better for him to have lived, even just in your womb, than for you to have never known him at all. Teddy has changed you in ways you are just beginning to see. I know, because my baby changed me. My life is so much richer for having had her—" My voice cracked again, and I swallowed. "Even for so briefly. She changed me for the good."

Ki wept softly, her hands still clutching mine. She nodded and let go just long enough to wipe the napkin over her face.

"Baby Tessia needs you now," I said. "She needs you to be strong. She needs you to take care of yourself so you can be there for her. She needs you to tell her about her brother so that his life can enrich hers, too."

She exhaled deeply and nodded again. Sitting up straighter, she looked me in the eye.

"Thank you," she said softly, still clinging to my hand. "What was her name?" she asked. "Your baby."

I smiled through my tears and thought of that precious baby I now pictured in the arms of Jesus.

"Her name is Claire."

Chapter 26

After my conversation with Kiya, I couldn't stop thinking about Ethan. My heart hurt for him in his grief in a way it never had before. Previously, I had only felt anger. He had gone to work the day after my surgery—the D&C to remove the remaining fetal tissue from the missed miscarriage my body had suffered. I hated the cold medical description of that, and my stomach still turned at the thought. It was an outpatient surgery. The doctor had said to take it easy for a few days, so Ethan set me up with medications and snacks within easy reach, turned on the TV, and handed me the remote. Then, with a kiss on my forehead, he left for work. Left me to sit in my grief alone.

The pain and anger had turned to bitter resentment, which I carried for months. But today, I felt different. I saw him differently. A husband—a father—weighed down by grief. He had wept bitterly with me when the doctor confirmed the baby had died in my womb. But then, afterward, it seemed he had moved on, shaken it off. What I now recognized was that he had tried to normalize our lives, to pull me from grief, to be strong. I recalled his frustration, the angry arguments, but even that I now saw through a different lens. He was hurting.

Hurting for me and for his own loss. Helplessly watching his wife waste away after losing his daughter, too. He grieved differently than me. That was all.

I knew I needed to reach out to him. I had been in Texas for almost five months, and it had been even longer since I walked out. He deserved some sort of communication, but I had no idea what to say to him.

I used my busyness as an excuse to put it off. Things never seemed to slow down at Mercy House. On the heels of Judith's celebration of life, I was busy coordinating a graduation for Nikki who would soon complete the program. At the same time, Judith was nearing her delivery date, and we were gearing up for new clients who would fill the empty spaces. Plus, in a surprise move from the control queen, Denise had asked me to look over applications, allowing me a say in who would be admitted to the program next.

Late that evening, after dinner had been cleared, I joined Sharon and Rick for our nightly porch time, but I still couldn't shake the thoughts of Ethan.

"You seem to have a lot on your mind tonight," Rick noted. Not prying. Not pressing. Just in typical Rick-fashion, he noticed things. I loved that about him, and it complemented Sharon's compassion so well. They had not pried into my past in all the months I had been here. Yet, I knew they cared and were willing to listen whenever I was ready.

Nodding, I turned my gaze to the wide expanse of lawn. "I've been thinking a lot."

"Everything okay?" Sharon asked.

"Yes." My thumb thoughtfully traced the woven wicker pattern of the armchair, as I chose my words. "I guess with all that has happened with Kiya, it's brought up a lot of things in my mind. And heart."

They waited for me to go on, but I couldn't bring myself to tell them everything right now. "I left things very unfinished in Boston. It wasn't fair to my husband."

I stole a glance at their faces, expecting to see shock or surprise, and maybe fearing some judgment. But there was none of that. Only compassion.

"It's never too late to reach out, Elle," Rick said softly, his voice barely louder than the rising sound of crickets in the trees.

I knew he was right. And I knew what I needed to do.

I stood up. "I'm going to head up to my room early tonight."

"You know we're here for you, Elle," Sharon said. "Whatever you need, just let us know."

I turned to go, determined now to make myself follow through with my decision. "Pray for me?"

"You got it," Rick said.

I glanced back to see him take Sharon's hand, and I knew he meant it.

* * * * * * *

The sun had slipped below the horizon, bathing my bedroom in a soft pink glow from the west-facing window. There, in the filtered light, I stooped to my knees and reached beneath the high poster bed to pull out my luggage. Carefully unzipping it, I folded back the top to reveal the tiny, gift-wrapped box alone in the cavernous suitcase.

My heart ached almost physically as I recalled the first time I saw it. It was January 12, the date that Baby Claire was due to have been born. I had already moved out of our apartment and was staying at my friend Julie's house. Ethan had come over, asking to see me, but I refused him. A pang of guilt hit my stomach as I remembered. He asked Julie to give me the gift. Angrily, I had tossed it into the back of my closet, unopened, as more tears consumed me.

I had been so warped, so out of sorts. It was hard thinking about it now as I stared at the tiny package before me. Willing the memories aside, I reached down and lifted it from the suitcase, carefully holding it as I took in the wrapping, the beautiful ribbon, and the miniature envelope tucked beneath. My heart pounded as I opened the envelope and removed the card.

"To Mommy with all our love from Baby Claire and her Daddy."

My eyes filled with tears as I pulled the ribbon and gently unwrapped the gift. Inside was a velvet box. Holding it a moment in my cupped hands, I took a deep breath and opened it. Within the velvet folds lay a dainty silver ring with a small, heart-shaped garnet.

January's birthstone.

I slipped the ring on my finger and held up my hand to examine it in the dusky light. Smiling softly through my tears, I whispered, "Love remains."

Swallowing my emotion, I moved to my desk in the window alcove and opened my computer, willing myself to focus on the screen before me. My fingers settled reluctantly on the keys.

"Dear Ethan . . ."

Fear and sadness gripped me, and a sudden film of fresh tears blurred the blinking cursor, causing it to dance in a way that mocked the remorse in my heart.

I don't know where to start, God, I thought-prayed, as a sob formed in my throat.

Start here.

The response was clear, but I had no idea what it meant.

Help me, Lord, I don't understand.

And then it came clear to me. I needed to start here. Right here in this posture of not knowing where to go, but willing to go nonetheless. Willing to reach out. Willing to humble myself.

My fingers flew across the keyboard, haltingly at first, and then powerfully as I poured out my heart about what God had done in my life. How I had changed. And then I thanked him for the gift.

Lifting my hand to gaze again at the delicate ring on my finger, I tried to imagine what Ethan must have been thinking when he went to the jewelry store to choose it. Had he told the clerk what it was for? Had he shared his grief with anyone?

I wondered what it must have been like from his perspective. Months of hell. He lost not only a child. He was pushed away by his wife. He lost a marriage.

Tears flowed freely as I typed, telling him how sorry I was for all I had put him through.

I looked out at the horizon, gathering my thoughts, then back to the computer screen. "Will you try to forgive me?" I wrote. "If you can't, I understand. I just want you to know I love you. Always and forever. Elle."

I pressed send, then snapped my computer shut.

You did it, Elle. The Lord's voice came clearly like salve to the gaping wound in my heart. *That's all I asked. For you to walk humbly beside me.*

A sudden peace washed over me, much like the first time I heard his voice speaking into my heart.

Thank you, Lord. I answered. *Thank you for being with me and helping me. We did it. It's up to you and Ethan now. Please touch his heart. Give him the strength to forgive. No matter what the future holds for us. Just help him to forgive. Not for my sake, but for his own. And for yours. Heal his wounded heart.*

Chapter 27

Judith's baby was born on the fourth of September. The big, old house felt strangely empty when she returned from the hospital. Nikki and Allanna had left two days before. Babs, whose baby was due in just a few weeks, was on bedrest due to pre-eclampsia. Even Serena and little Silas were quieter than usual. Kiya spent most of her time at the hospital still, and although baby Tessia was growing well, she would likely remain in NICU several more weeks while her lungs continued to develop. But the most evident emptiness was Judith's once-full baby-belly. It had flattened nearly back to normal on her sixteen-year-old frame. Two weeks later, I was helping her pack up her belongings.

"I bet you're going to love the transition home," I told her as I packed away the maternity clothes that would be stored for a new client. I had attended her initial discovery meeting with the family who would house and mentor her over the next six months. "Not only are the Lazaros an amazing family, but they have a pool! Who wouldn't love a house with a pool in this heat? Does fall ever come in Texas, by the way?"

Judith forced a laugh, for my sake, I was certain. "I have

no idea, but if it's like Shreveport, the first cool breeze won't come until October."

She fell silent again, and I realized my lighthearted prattle was too much too soon.

I could almost feel the heaviness of her heart.

"You doing okay?" I asked softly.

She shrugged. "Feels weird. So permanent." She looked down at her flat abdomen. "He's gone forever."

I reached out to touch her shoulder, at a loss for words. I knew what she meant.

She swallowed hard. "I know he's better off though. I couldn't give him the life he deserves."

Such maturity. Such bravery. Such selflessness. But I knew those words would ring hollow in her ears, so they remained unspoken. Instead, I thought of the universal language we spoke.

"I got you something to take with you," I said. "Wait right here."

I rushed down the hall to retrieve four neon-colored packets.

A wide smile spread across Judith's face when I handed them over.

"Trollies? For me?"

I knew that would do the trick.

They really are a magical fruit . . . or confection . . . or both maybe? Anyway, they should be added to the recommended food group list.

* * * * *

Morning devotions were a new thing for me. Each morning before the house began stirring, I crept quietly to the kitchen and poured a cup of coffee from the fresh pot Rick had already brewed. He and Sharon were always up well before dawn, and it was their example that had inspired me.

I sought out a new place to sit nearly every morning. Sometimes, the wide front porch, sometimes the settee by the back balcony where I could watch the sky turn from navy blue to pale purple, then glowing pink before the bright orange sun peeked over the horizon.

But this morning, I returned to my room. My heart was full, and I wanted a private place to share with God all that was in it. Ever since I had mailed the letter to Ethan, I felt a sense of freedom I had never quite experienced before. It was like I had come out from the shadows, from everything I had been hiding away and hiding behind. I had owned up to all the yuck that I was identifying with and truly felt the effects of a cleansed heart.

"1 John 1:9," I recited aloud, reading from the notecard on which I had written the verse I wanted to commit to memory. "But if we own up to our sins, God shows that he is faithful and just by forgiving us of our sins and purifying us from the pollution of all the bad things we have done."

I had looked up the verse in my Bible app and read it in several different versions before settling on *The Voice* translation to commit to memory. I loved the way it didn't mince words but laid out the truth in plain language that I could relate to.

I flipped through the collection of notecards I had made. It felt productive to memorize Bible verses. Much like I felt in vacation Bible school as a child, I gained a sense of accomplishment, like I was doing something important. Now, rather than earn a sticky gold star, I was eager to store these words in my heart to combat the swirling dark waters should they ever start rising again. These words were my lifeline. They brought me peace. They brought me comfort. They brought me victory.

I searched through the cards until I came upon the one I had titled, "Made New."

"Anyone united with the Messiah gets a fresh start, is created new. The old life is gone; a new life emerges! 2 Timothy 2:21, *The Message*."

I would send this one to Rae at the recovery center. She still had a ways to go to finish the program there, but she could receive letters.

I thought about what Miss Susie said about the love that was bottled up inside me, the potential I held to make a difference in the lives of other people. Rae needed to know she still had purpose and she could start fresh. God could do anything with a heart offered up to him.

The song, *New Wine* by Hillsong, began ringing in my mind and I hummed along as I thought of the rich words—words about coming empty-handed and longing to be filled with God's newness.

How true that was for me. And it was my prayer. I'm not the same person, I acknowledged. I had been made new. I felt the newness. What I had known about God was just a shadow of what I now experienced. He met me right where I was—in the midst of my brokenness, despite my position against him and all I had been taught about him.

"Thank you, Lord," I whispered, looking out through my window into the brightening sky.

Movement below caught my attention as I watched a gray Toyota roll up to the gate. My heart lurched. Ethan had a car like that. Lately, I'd been feeling sentimental when I saw one go by on the road.

And then my breath stopped short as I watched a lean man step out of the driver's side.

Ethan!

Did I dare hope this wasn't a dream?

I knew it wasn't.

God! You did this!

I watched as he stepped up to the gate speaker. And then I turned, rushing out of my room and down the steps. I was through the front door before I knew what I was doing. But I didn't stop.

My mind was a blur. I just wanted to get to him as quickly as I could.

I made it all the way to the gate before I realized I had forgotten to push the button inside the house to open it. But it didn't matter. His fingers wrapped around the scrolling iron work and mine reached for them, interlacing like they always had. His eyes were glassy with unshed tears, and my own words were lost as I watched his Adam's apple swallow back emotion.

"Ethan," I choked.

And then the old iron gate jerked awake. We both stepped back as it slowly rolled open. Glancing behind me only briefly, I saw Rick wave from the porch. And then I was in Ethan's arms, and he in mine.

A Note from the Author

Dear Reader,

I hope your heart was as touched by Elle's story as mine was writing it. Wish you could engage with ministries like the ones presented in this fictional story? You can! Mercy House, Moms in Prayer, CrossCounsel, and even Embrace Grace really do exist! While all aspects of the ministries may not be accurately portrayed, each are making an eternal impact on the lives of those they serve. See how you can connect with and support these important ministries by checking out the sites listed below:

MercyHouse.org
MomsinPrayer.org
CrossCounsel.com
EmbraceGrace.org

Since those are real places, you may be wondering about the characters. So, let me set the record straight: all characters are fictionalized. A few characters like Sharon, Kathy, and Miss Susie are loosely based on women I've known and admired for the amazing work they do in representing the heart of Jesus to others. And, as with most fiction, bits and pieces of stories of other characters came from snippets of real life I've either heard about or lived. Yes, some aspects of Elle's life are based on my own story. I know firsthand the pain of losing a precious child still in the womb. His life is no less significant than yours or mine, in spite of the fact that he never took a breath on this earth. Like Claire in the story, my Chet left his baby footprints all over my heart. Even though he was a brief 21 weeks in my womb, I am a richer person by far for having had him in my life. I credit him with having driven me into the arms of Jesus, where I found solace and strength to live.

It is to Chet and all those like him that I dedicate this story, those who may not have had the opportunity to make their mark on the world, but who definitely made their mark on those of us who loved them.

And one final thing that I desperately want you to know is true about this fictionalized story is the fact that you really can have an authentic personal relationship with Jesus. He wants that because he loves you. No matter what kind of history you have or scars you bear, he came to bring you healing and freedom.

1 John 3:20-24 is worth reading. It tells us:

"Whenever our hearts make us feel guilty and remind us of our failures, we know that God is much greater and more merciful than our conscience, and he knows everything there is to know about us. My delightfully loved friends, when our hearts don't condemn us, we have a bold freedom to speak face-to-face with God" (1 John 3:20-21 The Passion Translation).

That's exactly what Miss Susie encouraged Elle to do!

God wants a relationship with you. That's why he came to

this earth through his Son, Jesus. His direction for us is simple: "to continually place our trust in the name of his Son, Jesus Christ, and that we keep loving one another, just as he commanded us" (1 John 3:23). And by doing so, we will "know and have proof that he constantly lives and flourishes in us, by the Spirit that he has given us" (1 John 3:24).

Jesus and you! The constant companion and loving presence of God that will never leave you and never forsake you. He promised that he will be with us always (Matthew 28:20).

If you need a friend to pray with you for that assurance, I would be honored to do so. You can connect with me by going to the contact form at terrytamashiroharris.com.

May the peace of God which surpasses all understanding, guard your hearts and minds in Christ Jesus (Philippians 4:7).

Love,

Terry

About the Author

Terry Tamashiro Harris is a writer, editor, and publisher, whose passion for empowering individuals to grow in faith has been the cornerstone of her career. Since 2010, Terry has edited and published award-winning Christian non-fiction, helping countless readers navigate their spiritual journeys with grace and truth. Now, with her debut novel, *Love Remains*, Terry weaves a narrative designed to bring hope and healing to those grappling with loss and to affirm the enduring power of God's love in the midst of hardship.

Terry's life off the page is as rich and fulfilling as her literary pursuits. Married to her high school sweetheart, Wayne, their union is a testament to the strength of love and partnership. Together, they have navigated the ups and downs of life, celebrating successes and facing challenges hand in hand.

Terry and Wayne split their time between their hometown of Ada, Oklahoma, and their home base in Arlington, Texas. She enjoys traveling with her three grown children, taking long walks with her dog named Monkey, and lingering over a cup of tea while in deep conversation with friends.

Connect with Terry at terrytamashiroharris.com.

With Heartfelt Gratitude

Many people have contributed to the making of this book. I am deeply grateful for my encouragers—those who have supported me, encouraged me, and even pushed me at times. This list includes both dear family and close friends, but I do want to thank a few key people by name. Without you, this book would still be tucked away in the recesses of my heart.

I am deeply grateful to my prayer partners—those in my small groups and book launch team, and of course my mom, Melodee; to KT, my fellow writer who offered feedback and accountability; to Ginny, writing coach and developmental editor, whose stamp of approval helped me push past doubt; to Megan, for your careful copyediting and proofing, as well as your work on the publishing front; to Ben, artist extraordinaire, whose design talents and patience created a beautiful book; to Teo, my sweet son and plot buddy, who always pushes me out of my comfort zone; to Lauren, my precious daughter, whose excitement gave me the courage to pursue publication; to Preston, my firstborn, whose life brought a deep measure of healing, which allowed me to start sharing my story; to Wayne, my dear husband, who never doubted and always encouraged my writing, and who walked the true parts of this story with me—I love you so much. And, of course, to my Lord Jesus—this entire book is written for You, to share Your love—the Father's heart—with all who read it. What a joy it was writing this book with You! Soli deo gloria!

If you think others would benefit from reading this book, please consider leaving a review on GoodReads, Amazon, or your platform of choice.

www.ingramcontent.com/pod-product-compliance
Lightning Source LLC
Chambersburg PA
CBHW020113180626
46812CB00006B/2584